THE PUCK CHARMER

CATHRYN FOX

spot a guy jumping from his car, which looks a heck of a lot older than my vehicle, but thanks to duct tape and prayers, my girl is still road worthy.

Someone yanks on my door but it doesn't open. Why would it? This guy doesn't know Moxie's tricks—yes, I call my truck Moxie, because she's tough and tenacious, and will not go down without a fight. Plus, why would she open for him when he just rear-ended us? That is no way to treat a lady.

Wait, maybe that didn't come out right.

"Are you okay?" the guy asks. He tugs on the door a few more times, but his efforts prove fruitless. "I can't get your door open."

"That's because you don't know how to handle her," I mutter, and wait for my brain to stop spinning.

"What?"

"Never mind. Hang on." I take two deep breaths and when I'm no longer seeing triple, I reach for the door handle and yank it upward, giving it just the right amount of pressure to release the latch. The door opens and the next thing I know a man is leaning into me and I'm staring into the darkest brown eyes I've ever seen. Holy crap. Talk about swoon worthy. Then again it's possible my vision is simply wobbly because I'm close to fainting—the possibility of a concussion and all. Still though, his big brown eyes are like a steaming mug of hot chocolate, and the specks, like mini marshmallows, if they were gold, of course.

"Are you okay?" he asks, worry in those eyes as they move over my face with real concern.

"I banged my head."

"We need to get you to the clinic."

"Oh, hell no," I say, not only because I don't need a big medical bill, but because I need to get to Mrs. Henderson's house like five minutes ago. He opens his mouth to protest but I speak first. "Is there much damage to my trailer?" I put one leg out, and push from my seat, but when I do, I sway a bit.

"Whoa," he says and wraps strong arms around my waist. "You okay?

"Just give me a minute." I let him hold me for a second longer, but only because I'm dizzy. It has nothing at all to do with the nice way his hard chest is pressing against mine or the way his strong arms are so sure and supportive. Yeah, nothing to do with those sweet sensations coursing through my body at all.

Good God, I am so pathetic.

"I'm okay," I say and reluctantly escape the circle of his arms. He follows me to the back of my vehicle, and I examine the dent in my trailer. No big deal. The lights are still intact, which means it's drivable, so I'm good to go, and go I must. I turn to look at his car, and there is a nice buckle to his bumper.

"I'm so sorry," he says. "I pulled in and didn't realize you were backing up."

I shade the sun from my eyes and glance up at him. My God, he's like one tall snack. "Your car has more damage than mine."

"I'm not worried about my car, I'm worried about you."

My legs wobble again, but not because of the accident. Wait, did he just say he was more worried about me? I almost laugh. It's been a helluva long time since anyone has worried about me.

"I want to take you to see a doctor."

I turn and look at the plants in need of soil and water. "What I really need help with is getting to Mrs. Henderson's on time and getting these trees planted," I say under my breath, my stomach tight. If I don't make it there before she leaves for her spa appointment, I won't know what changes she wants, and chances are she'll fire me if I can't make her deadline. I have so few contracts on the go, I can't lose this one.

He takes his ballcap off and readjusts it over his head as he stands before me in a navy T-shirt and jeans, city boy written all over him. Did he take a wrong turn or something? Meanwhile, I'm standing here in dirty coveralls. I guess it's a good thing I'm not trying to impress him.

"I can do that," he says.

"Wait, what?" I stare at him, and he stands there like he's waiting for me to say something. Dammit, he probably is. Maybe I do have a concussion. Or maybe I should be paying attention to what he's saying instead of admiring his six feet of perfection. "You can do what?"

His eyes narrow. "Are you sure you're okay?"

"We'll have to discuss this later. I need to go." I make a move to step around him.

He blocks my path with all his deliciousness. "Fine, but you can't drive."

"You're not the boss of me"

Really Alyssa? You're letting this hot guy reduced you to a love-struck teen?

Apparently.

He scratches his face, like he's trying to cover a grin. Are you kidding me? I glare at him. "Are you laughing at me?"

"No, you're just kind of stubborn, and you kind of reminded me of my niece when you said that."

"I have a job I need to get to." I head toward the driver's seat, but my stupid vision blurs. I grasp for the side of my truck, but the big jerk catches me before I stumble.

"I can't let you drive like this."

"But I—"

"You're too dizzy to drive, and I can't let you go just yet, anyway."

"You can't?" I ask, my gaze dropping to his nice mouth, to

those kissable lips. Is he feeling this pull between us every bit as much as I am? Is that why he can't let me go just yet?

"We didn't exchange insurance information," he says.

Guess not.

I take in the state of his sorry, banged up bumper. "It's okay. I'm not worried about it."

He frowns, and looks at me like an apple tree might have just sprouted from my head. "You can't be serious."

I sigh. "Sometimes we just need a break, you know."

His eyes narrow in on me. What, has no one ever given him a break before? Maybe not, which makes me want to give him one all the more.

"I know, but—"

"Listen can we discuss this later," I say, having no intentions of exchanging information and making him pay. "I really need to go."

"Only if I can drive you."

"Your car is banged up and I need my truck."

"I can drive you in your truck."

"Moxie doesn't like strangers taking her wheel."

"Ah, what?"

I shake my head and instantly regret it when it throbs. "Nothing."

"Wait, you call your truck Moxie?"

Instead of answering, I ask, "Do you know how to work a stick?" Shit, that doesn't sound right. "I mean—"

"Yes, I know how to work a stick."

Dammit, I was hoping to snag him up with that one.

I'm about to protest again, all the while struggling *not* to think about him working a certain stick—clearly I need to get out more often—when he says, "What kind of a guy would I be if I let you drive after I hit you, and just so you know, I'm responsible for the accident, and I'm not taking no for an answer. I can be stubborn, too."

"Fine," I say, and circle the truck, climbing into the passenger seat. The clock is ticking and I have no more time to argue with this city boy, and when it comes right down to it, I have a killer headache and probably shouldn't be driving. "Let's just hurry." He fusses with the door some more, and now it's my turn to laugh.

"Something funny?" he asks after he finally manages to get it open.

"Moxie can be temperamental. You have to know how to handle her."

His gaze slides my way as he starts the vehicle. "Oh yeah?" he asks, a smirk toying with the corner of his mouth.

"Clearly you don't have the magic touch." As soon as the words leave my mouth, I realize how sexual they sound, I'm guessing from his smirk, he does too.

He arches a brow. "You don't think?"

I briefly shut my eyes. "I think I might have bumped my head harder than I realize."

"After we get you to Mrs. Henderson's I want you to get checked out."

"Yeah sure."

Not.

I stare at him. "Can we go?"

"You want to tell me how to get there?"

"Right, you're not from around here." I point. "Go left at the second set of lights."

He pulls onto the road, and I take a peek at his strong profile. He turns my way and catches me staring. Dammit. I quickly shift my focus back to the road.

"How did you know I wasn't from around here?" he asks.

I lift my chin an inch. "You would have known where Mrs. Henderson lives."

He chuckles. "I guess in a small town everyone knows everyone."

"Something like that. What are you doing here, anyway? Passing through?"

His jaw stiffens as he stares straight ahead. That's when it occurs to me that I don't even know his name. I could have just handed my keys and control of my truck to some out-of-towner with the intention of harvesting my body parts.

As he hesitates, like he's trying to figure out how to answer my question, I worry that I could be locked in my vehicle with an axe murderer.

I really need to stop watching scary movies.

"Who are you?"

COPYRIGHT

The Puck Charmer

ALYSSA

It's a good thing I'm not afraid of hard work.

Hernias however, yeah, I'm a little afraid of them and that's pretty much what I'm about to give myself as I lift the last fruit tree into the back of my beat-up work trailer. Do they have to weigh five billion pounds? Okay, maybe that's exaggerating, but who needs to hit the gym when they're a landscaping artist? I'm getting muscles on my muscles and that is such a lovely look for a twenty-five-year-old woman. I snort. Like there are any hot guys in this small Vermont town worth dating, anyway. All my friends—old boyfriend included—took off for college, or bigger and better. Me? I went to our local community college and studied landscaping design. I'm here for the long haul, even though six months of the year it's freezing cold and not good for a person who beautifies and redesigns yards for a living. But moving away is out of the question.

I close the trailer gate and the hinges squeal in protest. As I make a mental note to lubricate them when I get home, I wipe the perspiration from my forehead with gloved hands. A car horn beeps and I wave to my neighbor as he drives by. Old man Landry has been trying to set me up with his grandson, who works on Wall Street in New York. But I'm just a small-town girl and that's a whole different world for me. I sigh, tug off my gloves, and pull my phone from my back pocket to check the time.

"Shit, shit, shit," I mumble under my breath. Loading all those plants took longer than anticipated. My buddy Eli, who usually helps me with this task—and hires me in the winter during my dead time—is out sick, and everyone else was too busy with other customers. I move a little faster. No way can I be late.

Mrs. Henderson asked me to be there before eleven—before she had to leave for her spa treatment—and wants to talk to me regarding some landscaping changes. She's highly regimented, cranky on the best of days, and does not tolerate tardiness for any reason. I can't lose this gig. Not if I want to keep a roof over my head, food in my cupboard, and continue to pay for my ailing grandmother's care.

I step off the curb in our one-horse town, meaning all the businesses line Main Street, everything from Greenleaf Land-scaping, Foodland groceries, to Café Coco. If you need it, you can find it.

I slide into the driver's seat, press down on the clutch, and turn the ignition over. The car in front of me parked a little too close to my old truck—yeah, I probably should have retired her years ago—and since I don't want a fender bender, considering I have the barest of insurance, I put my vehicle in reverse, and start to back up. But suddenly I lurch forward, my head hitting the steering with an undignified bang.

Wincing, I put my fingers to my head, and lightly touch the lump already forming. Nausea wells up inside my stomach and the world spins around me as I put my truck into first, set the parkin break, and turn it off.

"What the hell?" I lift my eyes to my rearview mirror and

2

ALEK

ow, isn't that the question of the century? I don't want to lie to this woman. I kind of really like her, but I also like her not knowing who I am. I've never had this kind of anonymity before. Normally when I go somewhere, people are clamoring for autographs and pictures. I love my fans, I really do, and I wouldn't be where I am without them, but this, what's going on right here, even though she seems to have zero patience for me, it's kind of...nice.

I steal another glance at her, my gaze going from her dirty coveralls and mud-streaked face, to her mess of curly auburn hair all tied up into a loose ponytail. It's a gorgeous color, and up until a few minutes ago, I never knew it was my favorite.

I study the dusting of freckles around her nose, a few scattered on her forehead. Could she be any more adorable? Honestly, she's the antithesis to the women—or as we like to call them, puck bunnies—who travel in our circles. She's actually a refreshing break and I don't even know her name.

Nor does she know mine.

I suddenly realize she's gripping the door handle like she's ready to tug it and jump from the vehicle. Shit.

"Are you going to tell me?" she asks again.

I take in the worry in her eyes. My God, she's all hunched up in the corner acting like I might have just escaped an asylum. "My name is Alek Matthews," I say quickly, wanting to put her at ease, yet hoping that name doesn't ring any sort of bells. "I'm actually staying at my buddy's place. He's out of town and asked me if I wanted to house sit. He has a dog." I jerk my thumb in the opposite direction. "He lives in that big house, just on the other side of town."

Her eyes narrow in on me. "Are you talking about Tyler Phillips?"

I turn back to the road, and slow when the light turns red. "Yeah, you know him?"

"Everyone knows him." Her freckles bunch when she crinkles her nose, like she's deep in thought. She waves to the elderly woman crossing the street in front of us and says, "He's kind of a recluse, though.'

I tap the steering wheel. "Millionaire at the age of twenty-eight, thanks to the app he created."

"Yeah, but that was some popular app. He changed the dating game for women. Gave us all the control."

The light turns green and I accelerate. "You use the app?"

She snorts, like that's the most ridiculous idea in the world. "Nope. I just know about it."

I consider that for a minute. A girl like her must be taken, which is why she clearly has no need to use the app. Yeah, that has to be it.

"He rarely comes to town. I never see him around much." She eyes me. "Wait, how do I know you didn't murder him in his sleep and this is a cover story?"

I grin at her overactive, yet cautious imagination. "Call

him if you want." I pull my phone from my pocket and hold it out to her.

"No, I'm good." She waves my hand away. "You could have arranged a fake call, and I'm not making it my business. After today, I'll probably never see you again anyway."

Not if I have anything to do with it.

I set the phone down beside me. "Suit yourself."

"Does he get lonely all up in that big house by himself?"

"I think he likes it that way. I guess all the media attention got to him and he just wants to fly under the radar. That's understandable, don't you think?" I ask, curious about her answer, because that's why I'm here in small town Vermont. I need a break from the chaos and cameras, not to mention my parents. I love them, but after my brother got married and gave them a grandchild, they've been down my back to do the same. Apparently, they don't like my lifestyle or my on ice/off ice handle. The Puck Charmer. Jesus, I could kill crazy Cason Callaghan with a mean right hook for starting that one. Although, I do love the guy like a brother. I love all the guys like family.

Her ponytail bounces around her shoulder as she nods. "I guess I never thought of that before."

I shrug. "Why would you? You don't have cameras shoved in your face every day, right? Never able to be yourself. People wanting something from you all the time."

"Nope, I would actually hate that." She goes quiet for a long time. "I feel kind of bad that I never really considered his situation before. Do you think he might like a burning bush?"

My head rears back. "What?"

"You know a burning bush. I have a couple extras. Maybe he'd like one for his yard. I notice he doesn't really take very good care of it, other than mowing it once in a while."

I grin. Clearly this woman is naïve and innocent and has

no idea how things sound when they come from that kissable mouth of hers. A woman with red hair as lush and vibrant as hers probably shouldn't be talking about offering anyone a burning bush.

"I was thinking it might be a nice conversation starter," she says.

"Yeah, a burning bush is always a great conversation starter."

"Wait." She stares at me and her face turns as red as her hair. "Oh, my God. I didn't mean—" She shakes her head. "What is the matter with me?"

"You banged your head, hard." I say, giving her an out. "Things are coming out wrong."

"Yeah, that must be it." Her smile is so sweet, so warm and grateful, my stomach tightens. The last time I met a woman as genuine as her was...never.

"Do you know you have..." I brush my thumb over my cheek, and her eyes go wide. She pulls down her visor and groans when she sees the streak of mud on her face.

"Typical," she mutters.

She brushes it hard with her hand. "Your day's been going well, huh?" I tease.

She puts the visor back up and checks the time on her phone. "Yeah, best day ever."

It might not be her best day ever but it sure as hell is shaping up to be a spectacular one for me, save for my hitting her trailer and her bumping her head. But I never would have met her otherwise. I'll have to take extra good care of her to make up for it. Although she doesn't strike me as the kind of girl who lets other people do things for her. Like I said, she's different from the other women I know.

She gestures for me to take another turn. "Just around the corner here. Big house, pillars in the front." I take the turn and she continues with, "How do you know Tyler, anyway?" She gestures with a nod. "Right here."

I pull off the road, and head up a long, paved driveway, lined by shrubbery. "We both actually grew up in Boston."

"Oh wow. Do you still live there?"

"My parents and brother are still there," I say, hedging. When I'm not on the road, I spend most of my time in Seattle training. My summers are spent traveling or at my cottage on Wautauga Beach. A bunch of us all bought properties there. I'm supposed to head back to Boston for a week, but I've been putting it off. "What about you? Your family all still here?"

She goes quiet, her face paling a bit. "Yeah," she says quickly. "Park around back."

Okay, I've clearly hit on a touchy subject. Leaving it for the time being, I drive around the mansion and park. I glance around the massive yard. "This place is gorgeous."

She sighs. "It is, isn't it?"

"You're redoing the backyard?" I take in the huge swimming pool, the shrubbery, and the trees.

"I've done most of this. I have some trees to plant, and some shrubbery to prune, and..." She glances at her watch, her eyes wide. "I'll be right back."

She jumps from the cab of the truck and in the rearview mirror I catch sight of her darting around the house. I grin as I watch her go, and while those coveralls shouldn't be sexy, somehow they are on her. I chuckle slightly and turn off the vehicle.

I hadn't planned on bumping into anyone today—literally. The only thing on my agenda was to explore Main Street, grab a few groceries and keep a low profile. Damned if my day isn't looking up.

I adjust my ballcap and climb from the truck. The warm afternoon sun shines down on me and the water in the pool is a welcoming sight. I walk toward it, guilt niggling at me. Should I come right out and tell her who I am? I'm not used to people not recognizing me. Bending, I sniff the rose bushes and tension leaves my shoulders. This is exactly what I needed to help me relax today.

I wander around for a little while longer, and just when I think my new friend—she still hasn't told me her name—has abandoned me, she comes around the corner.

"Everything okay?" I ask when I see the frown on her face.

"Yeah, I just…" She wipes her brow. "I have a lot to do. Mrs. Henderson changed her mind on where she wants her trees, and now I have to dig new holes." I glance past her shoulder to see a big Rolls Royce cruise down the driveway.

"That would be Mrs. Henderson?"

"Yeah. Listen, I can call you a cab or something?"

"You think I'm leaving you?"

Her face scrunches up, like I just suggested we cook bacon in the nude. Although us being nude is not such a bad idea.

"Why would you stay?" she asks.

"I'm responsible for you banging your head. I'm not about to abandon you out here, in the heat…" I pause and wave to the trees in her trailer. "Carrying heavy shit like that."

"It's not shit, it's trees." I'm about to protest when she grins. "I spread the shit, or as we call it in the landscaping world, manure, down earlier." We both laugh and then she goes serious. "You don't have to stay, Alek. I'm sure you have much better things to do."

"You would think, wouldn't you?"

"What is it you do exactly?" she asks, her big green eyes narrowing as she scrutinizes me.

"I'm sort of in between things." Again not a total lie. I'm in between hockey seasons. "So it looks like I'm free and I don't have anything better to do than help you. We do have one problem, though."

"Oh?"

"I don't know your name."

"That's because I didn't tell you." She walks to the back of her trailer and opens the gate.

"You didn't want to exchange insurance information and you've yet to tell me your name. Are you in the witness relocation program or something?" I take in the wide expanse of yard and the greenery for miles. "Buttfuck nowhere is usually where they send people."

She laughs and whacks me. "This is not Buttfuck nowhere, and I'm here because it's home." She tugs on a pair of gardening gloves. "If you don't like it here, then what's keeping you. Move along, city boy."

"Captain Jack," I say, leaving out the part where I'm seeking solitude. "He's kind of counting on me."

"Captain Jack?"

"My buddy's Jack Russel terrier." Other than my teammates, no one has really counted on me or expected much, and I'm not about to let Tyler, or Captain Jack down.

She laughs, and the sound fills the air. "Clever name."

She tosses me a pair of clean gloves. "What are these for?" I ask.

"If you insist on staying, you're working."

I step up to her and touch her arm. Her gaze jerks to mine. "Seriously, are you okay to work?"

I lightly brush her hair from her forehead, and wince as I take in the swelling. "You have a bump on your head."

She shakes her hair back into place and shakes off my concern. "I'm okay," she says and I'm not sure I believe her. She reaches for the heavy tree, and I stop her.

"At least let me do the heavy lifting."

"Alek," she says, her voice so steeped in concern my

stomach tightens. I turn back to her and note the uneasy way she's shifting from foot to foot. "I can't really pay you for this."

Shit, does she think I'm doing this for a paycheck? Then again, why wouldn't she. I'm driving around in a beater I purchased a few days ago. I wasn't going to drive around in my sports car when I'm incognito. Besides, I have enough of my own money. I don't need hers, and from the looks of things, she doesn't have any to give.

"Then it's a good thing I'm not doing this for the money."

She angles her head. "Why are you doing it?"

"Because I want to."

She goes quiet for a long time, like she doesn't know what to make of me. After a while, she gives a slow shake of her head. "One more thing."

"What's that?"

"My name is Alyssa."

"Alyssa," I say, trying it out on my tongue and liking the way it sounds. It's soft and sweet like her. "Can I call you Aly?" I ask.

Her grin is cute, innocently seductive when she arches a brow and flat out says, "No."

3

ALYSSA

I steal a glance at Alek as he wipes his forehead with his forearm and puts his hat back on, covering his sexy mess of dark hair. His muscles flex and relax again as he wrestles the heavy apple tree from the pot and plants it in the ground. I totally get the appeal of a hot guy doing manual labor. There should be an Olympic category for this kind of perfection.

Even though it's my job, he sort of took over the second we arrived, refusing to let me lift anything or do any of the heavy work. Apparently, he's still worried I might have a concussion, and more than once this afternoon, I caught him standing a little too close, his gaze roaming my face like he was checking for signs of a head injury. For a girl who's always done everything herself, always took care of everyone else, his concern is throwing me off my game. I'm not saying I don't like it, though...it's just that it's confusing the heck out of me.

I lean on my shovel and grin as I watch him work. It's not my birthday, and it's certainly isn't Christmas—not even Christmas in July—so I can't help but wonder what I did in a past life to deserve this kind of help—from a smoking hot stranger.

He's also cute, funny, and strong—and so far, he's not really showing any signs that he might be a serial killer, not that I'd know the signs anyway and there is something about him that's trustworthy and puts me at ease. Strange really, as I'm not one to trust easily. The truth is, if I were in the market for a guy, I'd be all over that deliciousness. It's odd really. Rolling up the sleeves to help is the kind of thing I'd expect from country folk, not city boys. Maybe chivalry is still alive outside of Bridgetown, or Alek here is just an anomaly.

"How does this look?" he asks, and lifts his head to catch me staring at his broad back. I turn my focus to the fruit tree he's holding upright in the big hole he insisted on digging, while I filled in the others. When a client has a change of heart and wants to move things around, you move things around, despite the fact that you'd already spent hours digging up the backyard.

"The trunk is crooked. Move it a little to the right." I say. He readjusts the tree. "Mmm, I think you've gone too far. A little to the left now." He does as I ask, and I think it's still off kilter a bit. "Right again."

He casts me a quick glance. "If you're fucking with me," he grumbles, a playful look in his eyes as he gives the tree a little nudge.

I'm not normally flirty with guys, but I decide to play along. "What if I am?" I ask, and plant my dirty gloved hand on my coveralls. "What are you going to do about it?"

What do you want him to do about it, Alyssa?

"You really want to know, *Aly?*"

He's pushing my buttons to get a reaction out of me, and I have to say, I never liked it when people shortened my name —until now. "Yeah, I want to know."

His grin is so deliciously naughty my heart pounds a little harder. "Come on over here and I'll show you."

"I'm coming over there, but it's to plant the tree, and you can't show me anything with your hands full."

"Wait until they're not," he says, the promise in his voice teasing the needy spot between my legs.

I chuckle, loving the easy comradery between us, and toss the shovel aside. I hold his gaze as I drop to my knees in front of him. His eyes go wide and his throat makes a sound as he swallows. It's so damn loud it drowns out the bird chirping in the tree a few feet away.

"What...what are you doing?" he asks.

"Putting soil around the trunk." What the hell is the matter with him? Those gorgeous brown eyes look like they're about to pop out of his head. I shuffle on my knees. "What did you think I was doing?"

"Um...well..."

He swallows again and I instantly realize that I'm on my knees in front of him, my mouth perfectly aligned with his...*trunk*, I groan, and back up an inch.

"Oh, my, God," I grumble and grab fistfuls of the soil and start filling the hole.

Don't think about his parts, Alyssa. Concentrate on the job at hand.

Great, now I'm thinking about parts, and hands, and jobs, or rather hand jobs. What the hell is the matter with me? When was the last time a guy threw me off like this?

Down on all fours, I fill the hole quickly. I can only imagine I look like a dog digging for a bone. How's that for attractive? Not that I'm trying to impress this guy. He's a city boy who will be gone soon enough, leaving this town and everything in it in his rearview mirror. I pat down the soil until it's tight around the tree trunk. When I finish, I glance up at Alek, and catch his gaze moving from my ass to my face.

"You can let go now," I say.

"It won't fall?"

"It shouldn't. It's packed tight."

He lets go and stands back, giving his head a slow shake. "How the hell do you do this job alone?"

"With great effort," I say, and flex my biceps as I push to my feet. "And these."

He gives my muscles a squeeze and his grin is sexy when he says, "Impressive." I look over his body, but I'm the one who's impressed. Whatever he does—or did—for a living, must have been labor intensive. He glances over his shoulder. "What time is Mrs. Henderson supposed to be back?"

"She went to the spa, so a couple hours."

He arches a brow. "Want to jump into the pool?"

I give a fast shake of my head. "No, we can't do that."

"Why not?" He tugs off his gloves, and shoves them into his back pockets, giving zero fucks that their dirty.

"That's trespassing."

He grins. "You're a rule follower."

"Aren't you?"

"Usually," he says, "But you look like you could use a dip, and I sure as hell need to cool down."

"Even if we were allowed," I say, and walk back to my truck. I open the cooler in the back and pull out my water bottle. "We don't have bathing suits." I hand the bottle to Alek. "It's the only one I have. You don't have any cooties, do you?"

"Cooties?"

"You know, like germs."

"I know what cooties are, Alyssa, and no, I don't have them." He eyes the bottle before taking it from me. "Not anymore, anyway. Not since the antibiotics." His grin is playful, when he asks, "How about you?"

"No." How could I? I haven't been with a guy in forever.

He takes a long drink and hands it to me. I tip it and take a mouthful, and it's so oddly weird how intimate it feels to be drinking from the same bottle. The cool liquid coats my parched throat, but it instantly dries again when he tugs off his T-shirt to reveal hills and valleys that draw the eye down to the waist of his jeans—and a little further south, if I'm being totally honest with myself.

He turns from me, and I enjoy the view from behind equally as much, until I realize he's headed to the pool.

Panic invades my stomach. "Alek, don't." I hurry toward him and capture his arm. "I can't lose this job."

His face softens as he glances at me. "Hey, don't worry. I won't do anything to jeopardize your business, Alyssa."

When I realize my hand is still on his arm, I jerk it back. "Oh, okay."

He steps up to the house, and cranks the faucet until water pours from the hose. His grin is mischievous, and teasing as he glances my way.

I back up. "Don't you dare."

He turns the hose on himself, and his eyes drift shut as he soaks his body. His moan fills the air and I stand there like an idiot, jealous of the water dripping down his athletic frame. Once he's soaked, he takes a drink from the end and shakes out his wet hair.

He holds the hose up. "You sure?" he asks.

Dammit, he does look refreshed. "Let me wet my hair."

He steadies the stream, and I bend forward, letting him wet my head. The water drips over my face, and down my clothes, cooling my overheated body—which might have more to do with Alek than the hot afternoon sun.

"That feels good," I say, and stand. I take off my gloves,

wring out my ponytail, and wipe down my face. "A swim would have been nice, but…"

"My buddy has a pool." He shrugs. "Do you have any other jobs after this?"

I look around the backyard. "No, actually. This is it for the day. Tomorrow I have to trim the hedges and mow."

"You want to come for a swim?"

"Actually, no that's probably not a good idea, and I do have somewhere I need to be later tonight." I pull my phone from my pocket. "I should probably get you back to your car." I head back to the garden area and collect my shovels and rakes as he turns the hose off and coils it. With everything loaded back into the trailer, I'm about to slide into the driver's seat.

"Nope, I'm driving," Alek says.

I fold my arms. "I'm quite capable of driving."

"I'm sure you are, but that bump on your head hasn't gone down any, and until it does, I'm responsible for you."

"You just assigned yourself as my…"

"Doctor."

"Are you a doctor, Alek?"

"No, but I've taken enough hits to the head to know you shouldn't be driving, or lifting heavy things. You should be resting."

"Hits to the head? Are you a fighter or something?"

"Yeah, or something," he says, clearly not wanting to talk about what he does for a living. Is he embarrassed by what he does? Heck, he doesn't have to be ashamed around me. I dig in the dirt to put food on my table, and I admire a guy who works hard for a living. But if he doesn't want to discuss it, I'm going to leave it alone.

"How about this?" I say. "I'll let you drive me back to your car, and then I'll go home and rest."

"Do you have anyone at home to keep an eye on you?"

"No."

He jabs his thumb into his chest. "Then you're coming home with me."

"I am not going home with you," I blurt out. His face goes so serious, my blood slows in my veins. "What?" I ask.

"My friend has a huge house. Like huge. Let me make you dinner while you have a swim, and stay one night, just so I can make sure you're okay. You'll have your own bedroom and the door locks."

"I don't know anything about you."

He nods. "I don't know anything about you either, other than you're tough, smart, and run your own business." I open my mouth to protest, even though my chest puffs at the compliments. I like that he sees me that way. "It's either that or let me take you to the doctor."

I give it some thought. I really don't have the money for a visit to the clinic and would one night spent in luxury really be so hard? "Fine, I'll come for dinner, and a swim, but I'm sleeping in my own bed tonight."

He nods, and looks at his feet. I can almost hear the wheels spinning. He glances back at me, like he's come to some conclusion. "I guess I can stay at your place."

"You are not staying at my place, and I do have somewhere I have to be later."

"I can take you."

My God, this guy is so damn annoying!

Sort of.

Or not.

"Did anyone ever tell you that you are a pain in the ass?" I slide into the passenger seat and slam my door shut.

"All the time," he says, looking quite pleased with himself as he gets in beside me. He starts the truck and carefully negotiates the long driveway. I cast him a glance as he drives me back to his buddy's place. "What?" he asks, his peripheral vision far too good.

"Why are you doing this?" I ask.

"You gave me a break, and maybe I wanted to give you one too."

"I still don't get it. You accidently hit my trailer, then spend the day helping me. I don't know any guy who would do that."

"Then maybe you haven't been hanging around with the right guys."

ALEK

Alyssa's eyes go wide, scanning my buddy Tyler's yard when I pull into the winding driveway, and park her truck outside the three-car garage. I can just imagine she's redesigning the yard in her mind's eye. Honestly, what she does is hard work, and I admire that about her. Still though, I am a little worried about the bump on her head, and if I'm being completely truthful with myself, it's not the only reason I wanted to bring her back here.

I like spending time with her. She's open and honest and while I should probably tell her who I am and what I do—and I will—right now I'm just enjoying the ease between us.

Her smile is bright when she aims it my way. "This place is gorgeous." She unbuckles. "I'd love to get my hands on it."

There's a lot of things I'd like to get my hands on, too, but I'm not about to try anything with her. I so rarely spend time with a woman outside of bed. We usually hook up, and I offer her up a serving or two of the Puck Charmer special and disappear before sunrise. I don't want to do that with Alyssa and jeopardize our budding friendship. Outside of my buddies' wives, and Tyler's annoying sisters, I've never been friends with a woman. It's kind of...nice.

"Want to see the inside?" I ask.

"Oh, yeah." She slides from her truck and frowns. "Wait, what about your car? We can't just leave it in town."

"Why you think someone might steal it?"

She laughs. "You're right. I think it's safe."

I gesture with a nod and fish the key from my pocket. "Come on."

She follows me up the walkway, her gaze still scanning the yard, and I open the front door and stand back for her to enter. Captain Jack comes barreling down the hall, barking and excited.

"Oh my God, he's adorable."

"He knows it, too. He's a real player, Alyssa." I take my ballcap off and set it on the hallway table. "Has his way with the ladies, and if you're not careful, he'll have you rubbing his belly for hours."

"Do you like belly rubs, boy?"

He drops to his back, and spreads his legs.

"Captain Jack," I scold, and hold my hand up to block the view. "Cut it out, she's a lady." I wink at her. "At least he has good taste in women." She chuckles and stands back up. Captain Jack rolls over and whines. "You hungry, buddy?" I ask.

He barks and runs to the kitchen, coming back with his bowl in his mouth.

"He's so smart," Alyssa says.

"Actually, I think he's a bit of a smart ass."

"No, he's smart. You're the smart ass," she jokes and pokes me in the chest.

The gesture is innocent, but goddammit, I really like when she touches me.

I take her hand in mine. "Hey, I resemble that comment."

She laughs and when I let go of her hand, she smooths a few loose tendrils of hair from her forehead and glances around. Jack darts away and this time he comes back with one of his balls. I pick it up and toss it down the hall and he runs after it.

She's clearly impressed with the mansion, judging by her expression. "This place is huge," she says, and takes in the wide front entrance and long curved staircase with the dark wood handrail.

I put my finger to my lips. "Don't talk too loud, or your voice will echo off the walls."

She grins. "Will not. You're making that up." She whacks me in the stomach. I let loose an exaggerated oomph, and the sound *does* echo in the hallway. Her eyes go wide.

"Told you. Come on, I'll give you a tour."

"Wait, I can't look around. I'm..." She glances down at her coveralls. "dirty."

I expect another whack, when I say, "I think there's a hose out back."

She purses her lips, but there's a quirk of humor in the corners. "Not funny."

"A little funny?"

"No."

"Okay, how about a real shower?"

She crinkles her nose. "You don't think Tyler will mind if I use his shower?"

"Of course not. Besides for now it's my house and I'm allowed to have friends over."

"We're friends now, are we?"

"I mean after I rear-ended you, how could we not be? In fact, we might actually be engaged."

She nibbles her lips, like she's trying to keep herself from laughing at the sexual comment. "I don't have any clean clothes to change into."

"As they say in Jamaica, we don't have a problem, we have a situation, and that can be fixed by me lending you some of mine. We can toss yours into the washer."

I take Captain Jack's ball from his mouth and toss it down the hall again. He races after it.

"I've always wanted to go to Jamaica." She breathes deeply and lets it out slowly, her eyes dim, like she's dreaming of a different place.

"You should go sometime."

"It's on my bucket list."

"Yeah, I'd love to hear more about your bucket list, but first I need to feed Captain Jack here, and we need to shower." She stiffens...I kind of do too as I imagine the two of us naked under the hot spray. "Separately, of course."

She goes quiet for a moment like she's thinking about that. "I guess I could shower here."

"Hang on." I run to the kitchen and fill Jack's food and water bowl, and hurry back to find her kicking off her boots.

She looks uneasy about traipsing through the immaculate house—the housekeeper came this morning—and goes up on her tiptoes to follow me up the steps. I guide her into one of the big bedrooms. "This one has its own shower. You'll find shampoo and conditioner and all the hair product you need. Hair dryers and curling irons, too. Tyler keeps the place stocked."

"He has a lot of female visitors, does he?" she asks with a grin.

"He actually has five sisters, and they visit often."

She takes in the feminine touches in the room. "I figured there was a woman behind this room."

I laugh as I think about Tyler's big family. I always wanted a lot of kids myself. Not that I give marriage a whole lot of consideration. My friends are all getting married, but I don't see that in my near future, especially with the women I hang out with. But I have a big house in Seattle, much like Tyler does here, and I have to admit, at times it does get lonely. At least Tyler has his sisters who invade all the time, bringing their husbands and kids and filling the place with love and laughter. He jokes that he moved to a big house in the middle of nowhere to get away from them, and says he bought a mansion as an investment, but I know otherwise. He loves having his family around, and they're all vacationing in the Caribbean together right now.

"You're smiling. What are you thinking about?" she asks.

"Tyler's sisters." I roll my eyes. "They're so annoying."

"I sense a few stories."

"Many, but you need to shower." I step up to the window and she glances out before I pull the curtains shut to give her privacy, even though the house is completely secluded. "This room has a nice view of the pool."

"The pool is gorgeous, and that bed is bigger than my apartment."

I laugh at that. "You should be nice and comfortable in it tonight."

She plants a hand on her hip. "Alek, I am not staying here."

God, she's cute.

"Right, I forgot. I'm staying at your place. Do you have two bedrooms?"

She frowns and looks down. "Well, no..."

"A sofa?"

"Yeah."

"I'll sleep on that then," I say.

"Why would you do—" she stops talking abruptly, and shakes her head. "You know what, I'm just going to shower. We'll argue about it later."

"You know, I'm really good at arguing. I was on the debate team in high school."

"I believe you," she says.

"Jump in the shower. I'll grab some sweats and a T-shirt and leave it on the bed for you."

"Thanks, I appreciate it."

I look her over. "You okay, Alyssa? You don't feel faint or anything?"

I expect the death glare, but the sweet smile I get instead squeezes the air from my lungs.

"You're sweet to worry about me, Alek. But I'm good. I've been taking care of myself for a long time."

"I kind of figured that."

Her forehead crinkles. "Yeah?"

"Yeah. Go shower."

She walks away, and I dart into the room I'm using and riffle through the dresser. I gather her up some clothes, and set them on the bed for her. Then I jump in the master bath shower myself. I scrub the dirt from my hair and body, and once I finish and dry off, I tug on a pair of clean jeans, and a T-shirt.

I listen outside Alyssa's door, and when I hear movement downstairs, I take the steps two at a time and find her in the kitchen, glancing at the pool.

"Hey," I say, and she turns to face me, but the second I see her in my clothes, I nearly bite off my tongue. Jesus. My T-shirt hangs to her knees, and my sweats are so big, I could climb in there with her. Her coveralls did a good job of hiding her body, and until this moment I never knew how tiny she was.

"You're kind of like an ant?" I say.

"Excuse me?"

I chuckle at her puzzled expression. "That's a compliment."

"Yeah, I thought it was," she says and laughs, the sweet sound wrapping around my dick and squeezing. "Who doesn't want to be compared to an ant. They're a...oh what's the word...nuisance."

"I mean, you're just..." I motion with my hands, trying to say she's small. "You're little." She cocks her head and waits for me to continue. "And you're strong. You know like an ant, they can carry more than their body weight." Her lips turn up at the corner and I hold my hands up, palms out. "It's a compliment, I mean it."

She shakes her head, but her eyes are full of laughter. "I've been called a lot of things before, Alek, but an ant was never one of them."

I exhale a breath. "Can we start again?" I ask.

She puts her hand on my arm, and my dick twitches. "After today and all your help, you can call me whatever you want."

"Even Aly."

"Even Aly," she says. "But just so you know, that privilege doesn't go out to just anyone."

"I'm honored. Come on, I'll give you a tour." We leave the kitchen and I take her into the ginormous dining room, a table that seats twelve. "So why don't you like your name shortened?" I ask.

"Stupid boys at school. They used to call me Alley Cat."

"You didn't like that?"

"I don't think they meant it in a flattering way, Alek. Alley cats are animals that have been abandoned because no one wanted them."

"Okay," I say, and my chest tightens, because I suspect she's telling me something very personal. "I promise never to call you that."

I stand back as she runs her fingers over the long table, and glances at the pictures on the walls. "Oh my God, is that you?" she asks and steps up to a pic of Tyler and me, dressed in our swim shorts, no front teeth, and ice cream stains on our faces. She chuckles as she looks back to me. "It is you, isn't it?"

I groan. "I was seriously hoping you wouldn't notice."

"You were adorable, Alek."

"Ah, what do you mean *were*?"

She laughs. "Was your ego big back then or did you grow into it, like you did your teeth?"

"Excuse me?"

"It was a compliment," she teases.

"Yeah, it sounded like one." She examines all the photos. "Tyler's sisters were always taking pictures of us. One of these days I expect a blackmail letter. They were huge pains in my ass."

"You guys sound like you are so close. I love that."

"Did you miss the part where I said they were a pain in my ass." She grins at me. "I take it you didn't have siblings?" I ask. "If you did, you'd see things differently?"

Her smile falls and she turns from me. "No, just me," she says. "Do you have brothers and sisters?" she asks, and I don't miss the redirection of conversation.

"Big brother, also a pain in the ass."

"Oh, that's right. I remember you saying something about a niece."

"That's right. Trevor is married, and they have a daughter. She's sweet, unfortunately."

"What?" she asks, as we walk through the house, going room to room.

"It's a problem because now my parents are down my back, wanting me to settle down and give them a grandchild, a boy preferably."

"Ah, I see, and that's not something you're interested in?"

"Not really." Maybe if the right woman came along, but I don't come across those kinds of women every day. The kind I come across want the honor of sleeping with a professional hockey player. "I'm not really in one place very long either. Not many women would put up with that. What about you?"

"Well," she says. "I'm single, and that's by choice."

"Oh yeah?" My sweats hang on her body as we circle back to the kitchen. "Not my business, but I get the sense there was a douche-bag in your past."

She laughs at that, like really laughs, and I can't help but grin at her animation.

"I don't know if he was so much a douche-bag, but we just wanted different things." She looks out the window for a second. "Wait, no. You're right. He was a douche."

Laughing, I open the fridge to see what's inside and that's when I remember I was out on a grocery run when I literally ran into Alyssa. "Your folks still here?"

"No, actually. They're gone."

I lift my head from the fridge at the hitch in her voice. "I'm sorry."

"It was a long time ago."

Her comment about alley cats makes me want to ask if *gone* means they died, or if they up and left her, but I don't know her well enough to ask, plus I don't want to dredge up painful memories.

"That doesn't make it any easier, Aly." I sort of feel like an ass now. I've been going on about how much my family gets on my nerves and she has no parents.

"Everyone leaves," she says quietly, and crosses her arms across her chest in a defensive move. I'd be lying if I said I know a lot about the opposite sex. I grew up with a brother, and have no idea how women think, and I can't even begin to understand how they deal with deep emotions, but everything in that gesture makes me think she's trying to protect her heart. Who the hell hurt her?

"My grandmother raised me," she says. "That's where I have to be later. I visit her every night in the nursing home."

I nod. "Nice. I can't wait to meet her."

She shakes her head, like she's unable to process what I just said. "What are you talking about? Why would you meet her?"

"I'm kind of driving you around, remember? I'm responsible for you for twenty-four hours remember."

I expect a fight, but instead she rolls one shoulder and says, "If being responsible means you're going to feed me, then I'm agreeing. I'm starving."

"We might have a problem. I sort of don't have any groceries. That's what I was doing when I hit you." I pull my cell phone from my pocket. "But I'm a problem solver, so tell me, what's your favorite take out in this one-horse town."

"It's funny you put it like that. I was thinking the same thing earlier today."

"It's a nice town, though. I can see why you like living here."

She nods, but I get the sense there is more going on with her.

I run through a list of food choices. "Pizza, Chinese, Thai, seafood?"

"What do you like?" she asks.

I rub my stomach. "I like food, Alyssa. All food."

"Well, Benny's is known for their ribs, and mac and cheese."

"You had me at ribs." I do a fast Google search and pull up their menu.

"I'll go splits on it with you."

I gesture toward the fridge as I punch in our order. "Grab me a beer and we'll call it even. There's red and white wine too. Like I said, Tyler keeps this place stocked for his family."

"Beer is good for me. Oh, and they don't do delivery. We'll have to go pick it up."

"I'll go." I double check the order. "Okay, any other requests?"

"Apple pie." She moans, and I seriously wish she hadn't. The sound teases my dick, and while I want her in my bed—hello, I'm a twenty-seven-year-old guy—I also don't want her in my bed. I'm not sure how to explain it, and I don't even know if it makes sense, but she's different, and I just want to *be* with her.

"You got it," I say. I finish punching in the order, check the pick-up time and shove my phone into my pocket.

"I'm splitting it with you," she says.

I wag my eyebrows playfully. "Or...you could find another way to pay me back."

Her eyes narrow in on me, and I can only imagine what she's thinking—that what I want in return is sexual. "What are you suggesting?"

"Get our laundry going while I run out."

Wait, is that disappointment on her face? There's a definite pull between us, and an undeniable attraction, but she doesn't strike me as the kind of girl to jump into bed with a guy, and with her I don't want to be that guy.

Which is all kinds of fucked up, because I *am* that guy.

"Of course." She looks around. "Just point me in the right direction."

After I show her where the washer and dryer are, I grab her keys from the counter and toss her a grin. "You're not going to report your vehicle stolen, are you?" I tease.

"Are you bringing back food?"

"Yeah."

"Then no."

I laugh at that, liking her sense of humor.

"Feel free to make yourself at home, Alyssa. I shouldn't be long."

"I think Captain Jack here and I are going to walk the

grounds, have a look around and find the perfect spot to plant a burning bush." She drops to her knees. "How do you like that idea?" she asks the dog, and he licks her face.

"Dude," she says. "You have to buy me dinner first." As soon as the words leave her mouth, her gaze jerks to mine.

There's nothing I can do to stop my mouth from twitching. "Ah, so that's what it takes for a kiss. Well then, I'll hurry back with your dinner."

"I didn't…I wasn't…"

I tug on my ball cap, not wanting any of the locals to identify me. "Oh, but you did," I tease and she lifts Jack's bone and aims it my way. I dart outside and laugh at the sound of the bone hitting the door behind me.

I start her truck and head to town. I pass by my car, which is still in the same spot. I could call a truck to tow it back to me, since I don't want Alyssa driving just yet, but I'm pretty sure it's secure overnight in this town.

I park behind it and head to Benny's to pick up our order. The girl behind the counter eyes me, like she's trying to place me, so I tug my hat down a bit more. She goes to the back and comes out with a big brown paper bag.

"Thanks," I say, her eyes roaming my face. I get out of there before she recognizes me, and jump in the truck, strangely excited to get back to Tyler's place, strangely excited to know Alyssa is there waiting for me.

Makeup-free Alyssa with the cute freckles, gorgeous red hair pulled back in a ponytail, and coveralls that hide her body. A sweet, girl next door type who insisted on splitting the cost of dinner, didn't want to exchange insurance papers, and has no idea how sexy she is, and is not trying to impress me.

There's nothing I can do to wipe the smile from my face as I park and hurry to the front door. I push it open, and call out, "Food's here."

My voice is met with silence, so I close the door with my foot and head to the kitchen. I drop the food on the table, when outside I hear Alyssa's voice and I follow the sound. I catch her in the pool, swimming the length and talking to Jack, who's watching from the edge. She reaches the shallow end and stands, wearing nothing but my T-shirt. She wrings out the hem around her knees as the rest clings to her soft curves and round breasts, and messes with my ability to think clearly. My God, I'm just as bad as Captain Jack. We're both watching with our tongues out. When one working brain cell kicks in, there is only one thought rattling around in my lust-filled head.

I like everything about this woman.

5

ALYSSA

I gasp when I turn and find Alek standing there, staring at me with heat and hunger. I fold my hands over my chest, and dip lower into the water. But I have to say, I kind of like the way he's looking at me. When he suggested I do the laundry I thought for sure he wasn't interested in me, and while I don't want him to be, nothing could ever develop between us, there is a part of me that wants to stop being a rule follower, and just have a good goddamn time with a hot guy for once in my life.

"I didn't hear you come back," I say.

"Sorry," he says. His chest is rising and falling quicker, and I'd have to be a fool not to understand why. I'm in this pool in his shirt. My breasts aren't huge, but I could hold my own in a wet-T-shirt contest, and the man obviously likes what he sees. I like what I see, too.

"Did you find Benny's okay?" I ask.

"Yes."

I glance at his empty hands. "You got the food?"

"Yes."

"I should get out now," I say, more of a statement than a question.

"Yes."

I can't help but laugh as I take the three steps until I'm standing on the pool walkway, soaking wet and dripping on the tiles. Any other time, any other man, I'd cover myself, feel embarrassed about my near naked state, but the fact that I'm not, the fact that I'm actually standing here, letting him look is fill, is completely uncharacteristic of me. I mean, I hardly know the guy. What is it about him that makes me want to leap out of my comfort zone?

"Can you say more than one word?" I ask.

"Yes."

I laugh, hardly able to believe I've reduced this smoking hot guy—who could have any girl in the world and probably has had many—to one syllable sentences. I like it. A lot.

"Can you toss me the towel?"

He reaches for the towel and brings it to me. I wrap it around myself. "I really hope you don't mind me jumping in. Captain Jack and I were playing and it looked so refreshing."

"Don't mind at all."

I put my hand on his chest, and his warmth curls through my blood. Am I purposely flirting with him, teasing him? Yeah, I think I am. "Ah there you go, you *can* talk in full sentences." I look past his shoulders. "Now where is all that yummy food?"

"Inside," he says and follows me in. Captain Jack traipses in behind us, and starts sniffing and drooling at the delicious aromas filling the kitchen. He's not the only one. I breathe in all the delicious smells, and glance over at the bags. "How much did you buy?"

"Like one of everything."

"A big ego and a big appetite," I tease.

"I have a big everything."

He's grinning at me, and before I can stop myself, my gaze drifts down to take in the bulge behind his zipper. Dear God, what am I doing? He clears his throat.

"I think you need to get changed, Alyssa. Put on something dry."

His eyes are blazing hot and lock on mine. "Yeah, why?"

"I'm going to be honest with you here. You're giving me a hard on."

I chuckle, but do love that he's being straight forward, and there is so much tension between us, sparking off the kitchen appliances, denying it would be pointless.

"You change, and I'll dish up the food."

I walk from the room and dash upstairs to pull on a dry T-shirt, and tug the sweats back on. I make a quick trip to the laundry room and toss our clothes into the dryer. In the kitchen, Alek is nursing a beer, and the sight of him swallowing a mouthful gives me pause. My nipples tighten, as I imagine those lips wrapped around them, pulling on my peaked buds the way he's pulling on that beer. He sets it down when he sees me.

"Drink?" he asks.

"I'm a lightweight and I don't want to be tipsy when I visit Grandma."

"Sounds reasonable."

"This looks amazing." I sit across from him and look at the pile of food on my plate. "I'll never finish this."

"Just eat what you want."

I dig into the macaroni and cheese and don't miss the way Alek is squirming in his chair when I give a long, appreciative moan. I do it again with the ribs. When the hell did I become such a tease, but more importantly, am I doing it because I want something to happen between us?

Yeah, I think I am.

Get it, gurl.

Okay, who's voice was that and where did it come from? I chuckle and Alek's head lifts.

"What's funny?"

"When did you arrive in town?" I glance around the immaculate home. "Just today, or are you a neat freak?"

He laughs. "Last night, actually."

I nod. "How long are you staying?"

He glances at his food and puts his fork down, like he's suddenly lost his appetite. What did I say?

"You don't have to answer," I say. If he wants to keep things impersonal, I can too.

"No, it's just that I have to be back in Boston in a couple of weeks for Kaylee's birthday."

This time it's my appetite falling off the cliff. "Oh, your girlfriend?" I ask causally as I fork coleslaw into my mouth. Wait why is he grinning at me like that.

"You sound jealous."

I make a ridiculous snorting sound. "That's crazy. I don't even know you."

Oh, but you want to, Alyssa.

There's that weird voice again.

"Kaylee is my four-year-old niece, going on sixteen and I have no idea what to get her. She kind of has everything."

"She sounds like a handful."

"Oh, she is, but she's so sweet."

"Why don't you want to go back, then?"

He groans. "My folks. They're going to be on my case if I show up alone. Like I said, they want me settled and giving them grandkids."

"Ah, I get it." Marrying and having kids is not on his bucket list. I'm not sure if it's on mine either. The only eligible men in this town are scooting around in electric wheelchairs, or are sporting canes.

"For the record, Aly, I don't have a girlfriend."

It's a shocker really, considering how good looking he is, but looks aren't everything. Truthfully, I could see him being single if he was a complete jerk, but I'm not seeing that side to him either. Maybe he was hurt in the past and is off relationships.

"So this bucket list of yours," he says. "What else is on it?" I study his face, as he nibbles on a juicy rib.

"It's a big one. It's all written in my journal at home. Do you have one?"

"Actually, no. I never really think that far ahead into the future."

"There are so many places I want to see."

"Can I read the list?"

I shake my head. "It's kind of private, and you'll probably think some of the things are stupid."

"It's nice to see you have a high opinion of me," he teases with a smirk.

"That's not what I mean. You actually seem really nice." I glance at the food. "I'm being treated like a queen here, and after you helping me today, I feel like I owe you."

"You're under my forty-eight-hour watch, remember."

"Forty-eight? You said twenty-four."

"You're misremembering," he says, but we both know I'm not. He touches his head. "That's likely from the bump. I might have to up the watch to seventy-two." I'm about to protest when he says, "So what did you write that I would think is stupid? Swimming with dolphins?"

"Do you think that's stupid?"

"No, I think it's inhumane. We shouldn't be harnessing mammals for our enjoyment. I'm sorry if that offends you, Alyssa. I'm not going to go into a debate on it, or delete anyone from my social media because they have differing opinions, but it's just how I feel."

My heart does a little happy dance, and I really like how honest he is. That's so important to me, especially after my ex hid the fact for months that he was planning to stay in New York after college. I thought we were going to do long term. I should have known better. As a computer scientist, there's little to no work for him in this town, so why would he come back?

Oh, maybe because I was here.

But you're not enough to keep anyone around, Alyssa.

"I agree with you, Alek. I think it's cruel to keep them in an enclosure and make them perform."

"We agree on something anyway," he mumbles.

I laugh, knowing he's talking about his self-imposed doctor duties of watching over me. "I think we can both agree this food is awesome."

"Yup, and don't think this change of subject is getting you off the hook. I eventually want to hear all the stupid things on your list," he says. "Also, you have more food on your face than in your stomach."

My eyes go wide. "I do not."

He makes an exasperated face. "You're a hot mess, Alyssa. Go look in the mirror."

Still not sure I believe him, I say, "You have sauce on your face too. Right here." I reach across the table, and swipe his face, but when I do, he captures my hand. He glances at the sauce on my finger.

"So I do." My heart jumps into my throat when he takes my finger and puts it in his mouth, moaning as he tastes the sauce—or maybe it's because he's tasting me.

Holy hell.

A storm of need roils through me as we stare at one another, and I'm pretty sure neither one of us are breathing. His touch lights up my body, awakens every sleeping desire in me. Jesus, I'm pretty sure no man, not even my ex, has ever looked at me the way Alek is right now, and I'm also sure I've never wanted anyone the way I want him.

Captain Jack barks, no doubt confused by all the sexual tension, and I pull my hand back. I grab one of the napkins from the stack and wipe my mouth.

"So...uh," he begins and clears his throat. "You have to visit your grandmother?"

"She'll be expecting me," I say and wondering if he's thinking the same thing I am. We blow her off, and head right upstairs so I can blow something else off.

Good Lord, girl, who are you?

"Then we don't want to disappoint her," he says.

"You really don't have to go."

"You keep saying."

"And you keep ignoring."

He leans toward me. "Alyssa, I'd like to drive you to your grandmother's and I'd love to meet the woman who raised you to be such an..."

I arch a brow as he looks up and to the left, like he's searching for the right word.

"Amazing woman," I supply.

"I was thinking more along the lines of a stubborn, pain in the ass, ornery..."

"Ornery. Are you like a hundred? Even my grandmother doesn't say ornery."

"Well, if the shoe fits."

"Speaking of shoes. We'll need to stop at my place before heading to the nursing home. I can't wear my rubber boots in there."

"*We'll.*" He points a finger back and forth between us. "As in you and me?"

"Yes, Alek, you can come. I want you to meet her now. When my hair turns gray after *twenty-four hours*, this way my grandmother will understand Why."

He laughs, and I love this sound as it trickles through me. When was the last time I had such a fun and easy conversation with a guy? "You mean ninety-six hours, and I love the color of your hair by the way." His compliment silences me, as he stands and eyes my plate. "Did you have enough?"

"More than enough. Do you think I could give Captain Jack the meat from a rib?"

"That would only make you his very best friend, and we can all use a friend, right?"

He's right. We could all use a friend, and I'm pretty sure I made a very good one today. Tonight, however—and this is so not like me—I might want to change that relationship to friends with benefits.

ALEK

"Just up ahead, take a right."

I flick on my signal light and take the turn. Alyssa leans into me—back in her clean overalls—and I catch the scent of her skin. Still lightly soapy from her earlier shower, despite her swim in the pool.

"That's my parking spot right there," she says, and I ease Moxie into the big spot that also accommodates the trailer.

I take a look at the apartment building. "How long have you lived here?"

"Not that long. Just one year. After my grandmother went into the nursing home, I didn't want to stay in her old house alone." She reaches for the door handle. "It was big and lonely and always made weird creaking sounds."

"Maybe a pet would have helped." I bought my house as an investment, and the thrill of hearing my echo wore off in about thirty seconds.

"Then I'd be that old cat lady at twenty-five."

As I laugh at that, she looks off into the distance, her expression soft and...sad. "It's been on the market for a while."

"You don't want to sell it, do you?" I ask.

Her shoulders shrug in a non-committal way. "Just so many memories." She gives a humorless chuckle. "I used to think I'd always live in it, and raise my family there, and pass it down from generation to generation. But the upkeep is expensive and with Grandma in a nursing home..."

I get the sense she needs the money from the sale. "I'm sorry you have to sell it."

I slip from the vehicle and an elderly lady comes from the apartment, holding the door for us.

The lines around her blue eyes crinkle when she sees us. "Alyssa, darling, how are you?"

"I'm good, Theresa, how are you?" she says in a loud voice, but Theresa's attention is no longer on Alyssa. Nope, it's on me.

"Who might you be?" Theresa asks.

I chuckle. You have to love a woman who gets right to the point, and I guess at her age, why bother beating around the bush. "I'm Alek," I say, raising my voice to match Alyssa's. "A friend of Alyssa's."

"Oh," she says and doesn't bother hiding her approving smile. "We're all having trouble with the internet today," she says. "I think you'll have to nix the Netflix and just chill." My jaw drops, as her cane hits the pavement and she moves along the sidewalk. "Say hello to your grandmother for me."

"Did she just say what I think she said?"

I turn back to Alyssa, and her cheeks are fiery red, her jaw hanging open in much the same way as mine. Theresa whistles as she walks away.

"Yeah, she did, but I have a feeling she doesn't really know the meaning behind it. She probably thinks it just means hang out."

"I don't know, but I want to erase that from my memory."

Alyssa laughs. "You're not the only one. Come on."

I follow her inside her building, and we take the stairs to the third floor. She opens her door, and the warmth and coziness of her place washes over me. I grin as I take in the papers on the table by the front door and the scattering of shoes. It's like organized chaos and it instantly puts me at ease.

She kicks off her boots and I step a little further in to take in her living room and the stacks of books. "I take it you like to read."

"No, those books are just to impress guests."

"I'm impressed."

"Then it's working."

"I'll wait here while you get some clothes and your toothbrush."

"I'm not—"

"You said you had a sofa, Alyssa. That's a loveseat. I'd have to sleep with my knees around my ears." I catch her grin. "You think that's funny?"

"I'd kind of like to see that."

"Go. Pack a bag."

She takes two steps down the hall and disappears into a room that's likely her bedroom. "This is a small town, Alek. People are going to start talking if we stay together."

"From what I've seen so far, ninety percent of the population needs hearing aids, so they can talk all they want. No one is going to hear it."

Her chuckle reaches my ears, and she sticks her head out to see me. "Be nice."

"I'm always nice." She disappears again, and that gives me pause. I never stopped to consider her position. "Seriously though, are you worried about that?"

"No, I'm a big girl. I can do what I want."

She comes back into the hall with a backpack over one shoulder. "Did you pack enough for ninety-six hours?"

"I am not staying for four days." She puts on a pair of flat shoes. "Now can we go. Grandma is going to wonder what's keeping me."

I take her bag from her and open the front door. "After you, milady," I say and wave my hand for her to enter the hall. My chivalry gets me a big fat eye roll. We get back in her truck and I back out of the lot. "Where is the nursing home?"

"Take a right at the lights."

She jacks the music as I take the turn and I crank down the window to get a breath of fresh air. "It's so quiet here," I say.

"It's not for everyone." She turns away from me, but not before I catch a pained look on her pretty face.

"What do you do for fun, besides beautify people's yards?" I ask, wanting to bring her smile back and lighten her mood.

"I do love beautifying yards, and I was serious about the burning bush," she says. "I'd love to plant one in Tyler's yard. I bet Captain Jack would love—"

"To relieve himself on it?"

She laughs, and rolls her window down to create a cross breeze. It blows her hair across her face and all I want to do is touch it, rub it between my fingers as I place my lips on the pulse beating at the base of her throat.

"Okay, I wasn't going to say that, but you're probably right."

"So fun?" I ask, bringing us back to my original question. "What do you do?"

She breathes out and relaxes against the seat. "I don't have a lot of free time in the summer, but I love to...wait, you won't make fun of me, will you?"

"I can't guarantee it, Alyssa," I say with a straight face.

"Fine, I actually love to fly fish. My grandfather taught me when I was young."

My jaw drops. "You're shitting me."

"Nope."

"You're serious? You fly fish?"

"Yeah, do you think that's strange?"

"I think it's awesome. Will you teach me?"

"Sure, if you want." She reaches over, puts her hand under my chin and nudges it up until my teeth click. "But you can't have your mouth open like that. Otherwise you'll be the one catching all the flies."

I grin like a kid who just got a puppy on Christmas morning. I can't believe I ran into this woman, and she fly fishes. That's like the neatest thing ever. "What else do you do?" I ask, a measure of excitement going through me.

"There's a farm not too far from here. I actually love spending time with the goats, and sometimes I help out making the soap."

I stare straight at the road and shake my head. "You're full of surprises."

"In the winter, I ski, downhill and cross country. I make preserves from the berries my grandmother's friends give me. My grandfather used to have a snowmobile, and I loved taking it out. My friends and I would all go. Jonah's parents had a cottage..." Her voice falls off, like she's remembering happy times.

"I might never leave," I say, knowing that's impossible. My life is in Boston and Seattle and I'm on the road more than I'm not.

"What do you do for fun?" she asks and when I playfully wag my eyebrows in a sexual manner, she whacks me and says, "Besides that."

"I like hockey," I say, and gauge her reaction.

"I'm not a fan."

No shit, otherwise, she might have recognized me.

"It's barbaric," she adds.

"You're not wrong," I say.

"What did you plan to do while you were here?" she asks. "Netflix and chill?"

"My thought process is this," I say without missing a beat. "If that fails me, there's always fishing and making soap. I'm sort of a goat whisperer."

She laughs, hard, and whacks my stomach again. "You probably wouldn't know a goat if you tripped on it."

"I've had mutton before."

"Eww, I don't want to talk about that."

"What do you want to talk about?"

"Anything but eating cute goats." Her gaze drops to my mouth, and I suddenly get the feeling that Netflix and chill *is* an option. On one hand, I want that—I want it so fucking bad my nut sack aches—but on the other I don't want to fuck this, whatever this is going on between us, up.

"Right here," she says when I come across a colorful building with beautifully kept grounds, and elderly people sitting on benches.

I park, and we exit the vehicle. She frowns when I circle the truck to meet her. "What?" I ask.

"Grandma, she has dementia, so she might not recognize me at first. I just don't want you to be alarmed."

"Okay," I say.

Her smile is in place when we step inside and sign in at the front desk. "She would have loved to talk hockey with you, though. She and granddad were fans."

I adjust my ballcap, but I'm sure I have nothing to worry about. I've only been playing five years, probably long after she stopped watching. With my head tipped, I follow Alyssa down the long hall and into her grandmother's room.

The TV is on, some game show playing, but her grandmother looks like she's fast asleep. Alyssa checks on the flowers in the vase and plucks a few dead petals before sitting down. She gestures for me to take the chair by the window. I sit, and my heart pinches as I watch her. Her grandmother was obviously a very important person in her life, considering the fact that she visits every night, whether the elderly lady knows it or not. It's the sweetest goddamn thing I've ever seen. Alyssa takes her grandmother's hand, and I shift my chair just to be a little closer.

"What a day I had, Grandma," she says and smiles at me. "This city boy who barely knows how to drive hits my trailer. But no worries. No damage done to me or the vehicle." Her grandmother stirs a bit. "Then he actually helped me plant some fruit trees. He's a bit bossy and what an ego."

"Vincent, is that you?"

She gives me a pained look. "Vincent was my grandfather's name," she says quietly.

I put a supportive hand on her shoulder, and she tenses for a brief second before giving me a smile full of appreciation.

"It's me, Grandma. Alyssa."

Her grandmother's eyes open, and a smile touches her mouth when she gazes at her granddaughter. "Alyssa," she says. "I was just thinking about you."

"How's your day?" she asks.

Cloudy blue eyes shift from Alyssa to me, and I swear to god, I see a measure of recognition in them when her gaze zeroes in on me.

"This is Alek," Alyssa explains. "He's the one who accidently hit my trailer. Alek, this is my beautiful grandmother, Rose."

"As pretty as your name," I say and Alyssa leans toward me.

Rose chuckles.

"He's a real charmer," Alyssa says, and as soon as the words leave her mouth, Rose frowns, her gaze narrowing in on me.

"I know you," Rose says.

"Yes, it's Alek," Alyssa explains.

"Alek. The charmer," she says and looks down, like she's going back inside herself, searching for recognition, and my heart lodges somewhere in my throat. This is hard on Rose, but it's as equally hard on Alyssa, and while I don't know her, I know enough that I want to make this easier for her—let her lean on me a bit. Not only because I sense she's as alone and as lonely as her grandmother, but she's been lifting the load herself for far too long.

"Would you like me to read to you?" Alyssa asks, and reaches for the book on the nightstand.

"Yes dear, I'd love that."

Alyssa gives me an apologetic look. "I'm sorry."

"For what?" I ask, completely confused.

She holds the book up. "This might be a while."

"Alyssa," I say quietly, moving closer. "Take all the time you want. I have nowhere to be, and I can honestly say, there's nowhere else I'd rather be. I saw a vending machine in the lobby. Why don't I grab us a couple of coffees?"

"That would be nice, thank you," she says and the sweet look of pure gratitude on her face fucks me over a bit. Leaving her alone with her grandmother, I fish change from my pocket and walk through the nursing home. A few heads turn my way, but I stare at the floor, and only lift my eyes when I reach the machine. I grab a couple of coffees and head back.

Surely to God, her grandmother didn't recognize me. Didn't put Alek and charmer together to come up with my nickname The Puck Charmer. I shake my head. It has to be impossible. She barely recognized her own granddaughter, and even if she was still watching hockey, playoffs were over months ago.

I quietly slip back into the room and Alyssa doesn't miss

her stride as she accepts the steaming cup of coffee. I sit back and cross my foot over my leg, closing my eyes as I follow along, but soon realize she's reading a romance. I grin at that, finding this whole situation completely adorable. After about a half an hour, Rose's soft breathing sounds fill the room and Alyssa sets the book down.

"Ready?"

"Only if you are. I don't mind staying longer."

"She probably needs her rest." I stand, and Alyssa fixes the flowers in the vase before she leaves, and I follow her out. She's quiet on the walk to the car, and barely says a word as I drive her back to my place.

"You're a good granddaughter," I say when we reach my front door.

She smiles. "She was always so good to me." She places her palm on my cheek. "You were sweet to stay for so long."

That's a funny thing for her to say, considering I never stay anywhere for very long. Eventually I'll move on. I always do. This town won't be different from any other I've been in.

Why then, does that idea bounce around inside my stomach like a runaway puck?

7

ALYSSA

I awake to a bird chirping outside my window, and my mind instantly goes back to last night, and the way I tossed and turned restlessly in the most comfortable bed I've ever had the privilege of sleeping in. I couldn't settle down after a hard day's work. Likely because the hottest guy on the planet was in the room next to me, and my imagination was on hyperdrive. The only way I could finally get to sleep was to give in to my imagination and touch myself beneath the warm sheets.

Seriously though, long before we visited with my grandmother, I had every intention of seducing Alek. Neither of us were hiding the fact that we wanted each other—heck, he told me I gave him a hard on—but when we returned back to his friend's house, his mood shifted to mellow, and he grew quiet, so different from how he was all day.

The guy is definitely a contradiction, and I was a little confused by the shift in his behavior, so I left him to his thoughts and called it an early night. Maybe he doesn't want to start something with me because he's leaving. Maybe he thinks I'm the type of girl who's looking for long term. He'd be so wrong about that. Been there done that, and I know better than to expect anyone to stay.

I roll and wince at the sun streaming in through the crack of the curtain. I might as well get up and get an early start of it. I make a trip to the bathroom, tie my hair back and climb into a fresh pair of overalls. I gather all my things, and plan my escape, figuring I'll never set eyes on Alek again. I should probably be happy about that. Do I really want to get mixed up with a guy like him? Yeah, I do. But it's not wise.

My door creaks when I open it and I wait a second. With the all-clear, I tip toe down the stairs. Before I leave, I dig a few bills from my purse and put them on the table. I search for a notepad and pen and leave him an old-fashioned note. This is better than texting, and I don't have his number anyway.

Once finished, I head outside and jump into Moxie. I don't know why I have this strange sense of betrayal tugging at me. Maybe because I told him I'd stay for twenty-four hours and I'm sneaking out. But my head is perfectly fine, and I'm no longer dizzy, and he is not responsible for me. I've been taking care of myself for a very long time, although I have to admit, it was rather nice having someone care. I head home, and drive past his abandoned car on Main Street. It's a bit of a walk for him, which is why I left cab money.

Back at home, I head to the kitchen for a much-needed cup of coffee. As I drink, I make a list of things to do, and print off a few more fliers to hang at the garden center. While they're printing, I head to the kitchen to make a sandwich, and when I do, I spot my journal peeking out from underneath a stack of papers I keep forgetting to recycle.

I pull it out and run my hand over the cover. Mixed emotions curl through me as I crack the binding. It's been a long time since I looked through it. Starting a bucket list was a project in my senior year, and I've added to it since then. With another cup of coffee in hand, I drop down into the chair, and grin as I read through my list. A few make me laugh, a few I roll my eyes at, and a few are so ridiculous I wonder why I ever wrote them in the first place. Yeah, no way in hell would I let Alek look through this list. Not that I have to worry about that. I think I left a pretty good message when I snuck out earlier.

I jump when my printer jams, and tug out the mangled piece of paper. Once I get it going again, I make a sandwich and place it, along with some fruit, into my cooler, and head to Greenleaf to grab a few shrubs that were on backorder for Mrs. Henderson's garden. I pin my fliers to the board inside. I'm really hoping to get a few more big jobs like Mrs. Henderson's. They'll go a long way in paying the bills over the winter when times are tight.

My cell rings, and my heart jumps, but then I remember Alek doesn't have my number. My God, I wish I wasn't so excited thinking it might be him. I slide my hand across the screen, and have a quick conversation with Mr. Fraser, who needs his lawn mowed. I put him on my list of things to do, and go about grabbing bags of fresh soil and fertilizer. Fortunately, Eli is here to help me today. Although, after I ring in my purchases, I suddenly realize I won't need him to do the heavy lifting.

"Step aside."

My heart jumps into my throat at the sound of Alek's voice. I turn to find him tugging on a pair of gloves and handling the cart like it's his business to do so. I glare at him, even though my stupid stomach is doing some weird happy dance that might resemble the macarena.

Get it together, girl.

"What do you think you're doing?"

His look is pure confusion when his eyes meet mine.

"Loading this onto the back of your cart. What does it look like I'm doing?"

"Well, obviously I know what you're doing," I blurt out hoping I sound more frustrated than aroused, because holy hell, he looks good enough to eat standing there in his jeans and faded T-shirt, his hair a tousled mess like he jumped out of bed, and took off without running a comb through it.

"Then maybe the question you should be asking is why?"

"Okay, why are you so annoying?" I ask.

His lips quirk. "Nice to see you too."

My libido jumps into overdrive. "I didn't say I wasn't happy to see you," I say as he maneuvers the cart around me and heads outside. I finish paying quickly and follow him out. His muscles flex as he lifts the heavy bags.

"You don't have to do my work for me."

"I know."

"This is *my* job. My responsibility. Not yours."

"I know that, too."

"You don't—"

Before I can get another word out, he's there, right there, his mouth inches from mine. Air leaves my lungs at the intensity in his stare. He cups my elbow, holds me like he fears I'm going to bolt, and in a low, deep voice he says, "I'm responsible for your injury and for the next ninety-six hours I'm responsible for you."

"You can't be serious."

His breath gusts across my lips. "Would I be here if I were kidding?" His gaze moves over my face, checking the lump that has gone down significantly since yesterday and the dilation in my pupils.

I breathe in the fresh, soapy scent of his skin, and hope my knees don't give out. God, if I wobble, he'd likely add another twenty-four hours to our time together. Dammit, now I want to wobble.

Then why are you fighting this, Alyssa?

"I'm fine," I say.

"Yeah, you are," he says with a small grin, and I get the feeling he's talking about something else entirely.

"Alek—"

His eyes go soft when I say his name. "I'm helping, whether you want it or not." He shrugs. "You probably won't even know I'm here."

I doubt that.

"You were right when you said you were stubborn," I mumble.

"You're one to talk."

"Are you sure I'm not keeping you from something? I'm guessing you have better things to do."

"Is this it?" he asks and tosses the last bag of soil onto the pile. I nod and he steps close again, humor gone from his eyes. That intensity is back tenfold and a quiver moves through me. "You were gone when I woke up. It worried me."

My heart pounds and I struggle to form a thought at the raw way he's looking at me, need and hunger evident in his gaze. I'm sure my face mirrors his. This tension between us, my God, if we stand too close to the fertilizer, I fear we might detonate it.

"I didn't mean to worry you. It wasn't my intention. You just did so much for me already."

His eyes narrow. "Why did you leave money?"

I wave my hand toward his abandoned vehicle. "Your car. I didn't want you to have to walk."

He goes completely silent, and something that looks like astonishment pools in his eyes. "Jesus," he mumbles and scrubs the sexy scruff on his face. "You didn't have to do that."

"I know," I say with a grin throwing his words back at him and hoping to lighten the mood.

He grins. "I'm here to work, Aly," he says, his voice so low and sexy it strokes my nether region. "So work me."

Oh, God, do *not* think about the way you could 'work' him.

Too late.

But he clearly doesn't want to start anything with me.

"Yeah, okay," I croak out. "We need to finish Mrs. Henderson's lawn and then I need to go to the storage shed to get the lawn mower."

"Okay." He holds his hand out, and I stare at it.

"What?"

He shakes his head. "See, I was right."

"About?"

"You're still not thinking straight. Good thing I showed up when I did."

He's probably right. I'm not thinking straight, but how is a girl supposed to keep her wits about her when he's so goddamn hot, and helpful, and just so...everything.

"Keys," he says, like I took a good hit to the head, and it's messing with my memory. I'm about to protest when he says, "I've already proven I know how to handle her." His knuckles brush mine, and a hard quiver moves through me. "I actually think she might like my touch."

Holy freaking Lord.

She does.

She totally does.

But he's not talking about me, is he?

Then again, maybe he is.

"Fine." I plunk the keys into his palm and storm off like I'm pissed off. But I'm not. I'm a completely independent woman who can take care of herself, but secretly likes it when he goes all alpha on me and shows concern. "You are so annoying," I mumble, which earns me a chuckle.

He slides into the truck beside me and pulls onto the

road, already knowing his way to Mrs. Henderson's. He glances overhead. "I'm not so sure you're going to be able to mow that lawn after we get the soil spread."

We.

Is it weird how I like the sound of that?

Yes, of course it is, Alyssa.

"Looks like rain."

I lean forward, and crinkle my nose. "Yeah, I checked the forecast earlier, and it's not great."

"What do you do on rainy days if you can't work?"

"Sometimes I read, or sketch designs."

"Really? I'd love to see them, and I still want to see this bucket list of yours." He casts me a quick glance.

"I'll show you mine if you show me yours," I say, and then slap my hand to my forehead. "I think that came out wrong."

"I have no problem showing you mine," he says and taps the steering wheel like he just made the winning touchdown, or maybe in his case since he loves hockey, the winning goal.

"Is it called goals in hockey?" I ask.

"What?" he asks, laughter in his voice.

"My ex was on the football team in high school, so I've watched that and know it's called a touchdown, but I don't really know much about hockey."

"Yes, it's a goal," he says and turns from me, but not before I miss the agitation on his face, but why would he be upset? It's summer, so maybe he's missing playing or something.

"Maybe you could teach me. I've seen the kids in the neighborhood play street hockey."

"You want to learn?"

"Something fun to do on a rainy day. Maybe we can pick up some sticks," I say, even though I think Mr. Landry has a bunch. His kids played, his grandkids played, and now his great grandkids still play.

"I do have to go to the mall." He cringes. "Please tell me what to buy for a five-year-old girl."

I pull out my phone. "I'm on it, but we don't have a big mall here. I'm sure we can still find something for her."

His smile is so appreciative and sweet, my heart does a little happy dance that I can do something for him in return, considering all he's doing for me. I study his profile as he drives, let my gaze roam lower, to admire all six feet of muscle and testosterone. Yeah, I bet there are all kinds of things I can do for him in return. Things that are way more fun than shopping. Things that are dirty, and delicious and exciting. He's a nice guy. Like super nice. My guess is he's worried about starting something when he has no intentions of sticking around. Maybe later tonight, I'll show him he has nothing to worry about. Yeah, tonight with my hands and my mouth...

"Something on your mind, Aly?"

"Nothing much," I say.

"So you're agreeing to the next one hundred and twenty hours with me then?"

8

ALEK

Alyssa's laugh curls around me as I park her truck and we dash into her apartment. We just finished mowing the lawn, and getting her mower back into her storage shed when the skies opened up. Now we're headed to her place to pack, because yeah, I think I talked her into spending the next five days with me.

A measure of guilt niggles at me as we hurry to her apartment. Omission is the same as lying, right? And she's the kind of girl who appreciates the truth. I know I should tell her who I am and what I really do. Hell, she left cab money for me for Christ's sake, which is the sweetest fucking thing anyone has ever done for me. Although sharing her lunch with me is pretty damn high on the list too. But the longer we're together, the more we get to know each other, what I do for a living—and the fact that I didn't tell her—becomes a much bigger issue.

Shit. This is wrong. I know it. I can't help but worry, though, worry that the second I tell her it will change things between us and make her look at me differently. I've seen the reaction many times, and call me a fucking coward, but I'm afraid to open my mouth and ruin what we have here, because yeah, I like her, and I like the way she looks at me.

Last night... Jesus Christ last night I wanted her. In my arms, and in my bed. I wanted to put my mouth all over her, but I stopped myself. I honestly never knew I had such restraint, but once I sleep with a woman it's over. I'm here for the next couple weeks and I kind of want to spend them with her.

Will sex ruin that?

Can I take a chance?

She's breathing hard and still laughing by the time we get inside her place. I reach out, brush a wet strand of hair from her forehead. She instantly goes quiet, her eyes locking with mine, and in that moment, all I can think about is kissing her. If I start, I won't be able to stop.

"I'm wet," she whispers and a groan catches in my throat. Her innocence and the way she blurts out things that can be construed sexually is seriously fucking with me. She briefly shuts her eyes and shakes her head as she backs up. "From the rain, I mean."

"I know what you mean," I say.

"Let me get a quick shower and change into dry clothes. Go get yourself a beer."

I walk through her cozy apartment, and open the fridge. "Do you want one?" I call out.

"Sure," she says, and I listen to her rustle around inside her room. I take two beers from the fridge and twist off the caps. After opening a few cupboards, I find a glass and pour hers in.

A stack of papers on the table catch my eye as I tip the beer to my mouth. Plunking myself down, I'm about to riffle through them when a leather-bound book, spread wide open catches my eyes. I scan the list, and can't fucking believe it. I read through the entire thing, and I'm so engrossed, I don't hear Alyssa entering the kitchen.

"Ohmigod, no," she says and dives at the book, but it's too late. "You weren't supposed to see that."

"Then maybe you shouldn't have left it here." The clean scent of her skin fills my senses, and the sight of her in a T-shirt and frayed jean shorts grips my dick and tugs.

"I forgot I did," she says.

"I don't know, Alyssa. I'm not sure Freud would agree with you." A hot pink invades her cheeks and I cut her some slack by saying, "One of the things on my bucket list is sex while skydiving." I touch her book. "What you have in here is much tamer."

She covers her face. "How mortifying."

I remove her hands, and my heart squeezes tight. "Hey, don't be embarrassed with me."

She frowns. "You just read my ridiculous list."

"I thought we agreed, you show me yours and I'll show you mine." I reach for her, drag her to me, gauging her reaction. The air around us charges with sexual tension, and she shifts between my spread legs. I hold her hips and her head dips, her eyes blazing, matching the firestorm of need inside me.

After a long moment, she finally says, "I do believe that was the agreement, and now that you've seen mine..." Her voice is low and full of desire, telling me everything I need to know. I grin at her, and since we're no longer talking about bucket lists—and if we were, getting her naked would be on the top of my list—I stand.

She tugs at the bottom of my wet T-shirt. "Show me," she says, and I reach behind my back and peel off my shirt. Her gaze goes to my bare chest.

"Your turn," I say, and her gaze lifts to mine. She hesitates, and for a second I wonder if she's changed her mind, but then she steps back, and in one fluid movement, removes her shirt, giving me a beautiful view of her creamy cleavage, and pink nipples straining against a pretty lace bra.

"Now you."

I grin at her, and release the button on my pants. I shove them down and kick them away, and her gaze drops to the bulge in my boxers. I wave my hand, giving her the floor, so to speak, and she slowly unbuttons her shorts and lets them fall to her feet. I suck in a fast breath. She's so fucking sweet and sensual, and I'm not even sure she knows it.

"You're beautiful," I say, and she smiles at me.

"You're not so bad yourself."

"I like the idea of showing, but I need my mouth on you, Aly," I say, my voice low and deep, barely audible over the pounding of my heart.

Her breathing changes. "What a coincidence."

"Oh."

"Yeah, I need your mouth on me too."

She gasps as I scoop her up and carry her to her bedroom. I set her down beside her bed, and her hands move to my shoulders. I groan as she touches me, and I dip my head, dying to put my mouth on hers. She wets her bottom lip and my dick twitches, presses against her body, and I press my lips to hers. She's so damn sweet. I breathe deeply, and sink my fingers into her long, wet hair, tugging a bit so her head tilts more and I can taste the depths of her.

I finally break the kiss, and she writhes against me, her hard nipples scraping my chest in mind-fucking ways. In one quick flick, I have her bra undone, and she shimmies out of it. She steps back and toys with the elastic band on her panties. Damned if I don't like this sexy, playful side of her.

"About this mouth of yours," she teases.

I growl and step into her, cupping her beautiful breasts with my hands. Her body softens against mine, and I dip my head to take one hard nub into my mouth. I suck deep, swirl my tongue, and slide one hand down her back to cup her ass.

"God, Alek," she moans, her warm fingers raking through my hair, and I bite back a chuckle as she holds my head in place, a new kind of desperation about her.

Without removing my mouth from her breast, I back her up and carefully fall over her on the bed. Her legs widen and it's amazing how well I fit between them. I give one last kiss to her breast and lift my head. Green eyes full of desire meet mine as I shift her to the middle of the bed.

I go to my side, run my hand between her breasts and then lower on her stomach as I drink in the near-naked sight of her. My finger stop when I reach the band of her panties, but I'm not quite ready to remove them. I curl my finger in the elastic and tug. Her resulting groan lets me know I've hit the right spot.

"Spread your legs for me," I say, and she does. I slide my hand up her thigh, so hot from her shower, and from what I'm doing to her. I lightly stroke her through her panties, a taunting little touch that has her calling my name and lifting her hips from the bed. "You like that, Aly?"

"Yes," she says.

"Is this sweet little pussy aching to be touched?"

She audibly gulps as she nods.

"Last night, I wanted to fuck you," I admit.

"Why...why didn't you?"

"Because I like hanging out with you." I tug her panties to the side to expose her pink wetness, and my cock throbs. It takes everything I have to form a coherent sentence. "I don't normally hang out with a girl after sex, and the truth is, I kind of like hanging out with you, so I didn't want to fuck things up. But that doesn't mean I didn't want to fuck you."

She nods like she totally understands. "I like hanging out with you too," she says. "I don't think sex will fuck that up."

"Does that mean I get the five days I asked for?" Her eyes fall shut when I rub my thumb over her engorged clit and insert my finger up to the first knuckle. I still inside her, and she shifts trying to force me in deeper.

"Five days?" she asks, her body so hot and needy she's clearly not thinking straight. "What do you mean?"

"I rear-ended you, and for the next five days your mine to take care of." I inch my finger out. "Say yes."

Her hips lift. "You don't play fair, Alek."

I chuckle at that and slide my finger in deeper. "I play to win."

"One condition," she says, her breaths coming fast as I toy with her clit, and lean forward to run the soft blade of my tongue over her nipple.

"What might that be?"

"We get to do this every day."

"That's not a condition, Aly. That's a given. Before our five days are over, I'm going to own every inch of your body."

Her body trembles beneath me. "No commitment, no expectations," she adds and while I can't give her any of those things, for some odd reason her words sting.

"Deal," I say, and she grips the bedding and tugs as I slip another finger inside her.

"Take me," she whimpers.

She's so wet, and so close, but I'm not ready for her to come yet. I finger fuck her a few more times, and she cries when I remove my hand and skim it down her thighs, leaving a trail that my mouth will soon follow.

"No, please," she says, her eyes wide and wild with desire as her needy voice vibrates through me and massages my aching cock. "I need to come." Jesus, I love the way I can drive her crazy. But she's not the only one in the room close to losing it.

I press a kiss to her stomach. "I'm going to take you where you need to go, Aly. With my mouth on you."

A sound of pure pleasure rumbles in her chest. "Right, yes," she says, her voice nothing but a whimper as I relentlessly tease her. I purposely nudge her clit as I reposition my body and climb between her legs, her tight bundle of nerves practically throbbing against my fingertip. I glance at her damp panties, the treasure beneath mine for the taking. And I plan to take. Oh yeah, I plan to fuck this sweet woman until the neighbors can hear her screaming my name.

"I need these panties gone," I say and grip her legs and close them tightly. She goes up on her elbows, her beautiful breasts on display as I tug her panties down. With my mouth inches from her pussy, I breathe in her aroused scent.

Jesus, she's going to be the sweetest thing I've ever tasted.

She struggles to open her legs again, but I put my knees on either side of hers, preventing her from spreading. I press my finger to her clit and slide it down, parting her damp folds and licking through her wetness. I'm rewarded with a sweet moan.

"I love how wet you are for me." I stroke her and watch her find pleasure as I restrain her beneath me. "I'm going to make you even wetter with my tongue, then you're going to come all over me, Aly." I push my finger into her hot, tight hole and her muscles clench. "You need my cock," I state. "You want me to fuck you, Aly?"

I move my finger in and out, and nearly shoot off at her tortured moans.

"Yes, just like that," she says, as I bring her higher and higher. Her hands go to her breasts and she cups them, squeezes her nipples, and it's pretty much more than I can take. I drop to the mattress, spread her legs wide, and lick a path up her damp thighs until I reach her pussy. Her juices glisten beneath my gaze, and I dive in, take her throbbing clit into my mouth as I scissor two fingers inside her until she's practically convulsing beneath me.

My cock throbs, thick and impatient, needing to feel her wrapped around it in the worst way. She squirms and I use the tip of my tongue to apply pressure to her clit, wanting her to revel in every hard lap, even the littlest of sensation, until her body gives in to the pleasure.

"Yes," she says and grips my head, her hips jerking up and down as I lick, and nibble, and eat my fill. "Alek," she cries, and seconds later she bursts around my fingers, her hot flood of desire filling my mouth and dripping down my hands. I lap at her, drink her in, not wanting to miss a single droplet. I stay there until her body comes back, her spasms slowing, and I trail my tongue around her sweet opening, licking her softly.

"Jesus, you taste good," I murmur from between her legs. Inching back, I kiss a wet path up her body, stopping to tease her nipples again, and bury my mouth in the sweet hollow of her throat. My cock presses against her center, eager to get inside.

I rock against her, and rotate my hips. "Tell me what you want."

"I want your cock," she says, her nails scraping over my back. "I want you to fuck me."

"I need to get a condom," I say, remembering I left my pants in the kitchen.

"My nightstand," she says.

I reach over, not wanting to break the connection and search her nightstand. Eager, I start pulling things out, desperate to find the condoms. My fingers connect with something soft and long, and because it's in my way, I snatch it, and set it on the nightstand.

"Oh, God," she says, and I follow her gaze to the vibrator I just found. Shit, I hadn't meant to embarrass her.

"It's okay, Aly. I masturbate too. Nothing wrong with that and if we're being honest here, I masturbated last night."

She chuckles. "Okay, yeah, so did I."

"You used your fingers?" I ask.

She nods.

"I'd like to see that, you know. Right now, though, my cock needs to be inside you."

I scrounge until I find a box of unopened condoms. I rip into it. "I do like a girl who is prepared," I say, even though she doesn't strike me as the kind to sleep around. Not that there is anything wrong with that, as long as she's practicing safe sex.

"I uh...they might be outdated," she says.

"Shit, really?"

"It's been a while."

"Yeah," I say, and rub the back of my hand over her face. "I'm sorry."

She shrugs. "It's okay. I get by."

I grin at that. "Is it weird that I'm glad I'm the guy you chose to break your dry spell with?"

"Well it was either you or Ralph from 309. He's been hitting on me."

"Why didn't you go for it?" I ask, even though I don't want to picture her in bed with anyone but me. Not that I have that right or any claim to her. But the thought is a bit disconcerting, considering I never had one like it before.

"Because he's ninety, and senile and thinks I'm his ex-wife."

I can't help but laugh at that. "That's funny."

She chuckles. "I'm glad you think so."

Her hand slides down. She takes me in her palm and I forget everything. I forget that I'm in bed with a sweet, small town girl who doesn't know who I really am, that I've never quite wanted anyone the way I want her, and that while I only ever want one night, I'm not sure five days will be enough when it comes to her. But I forget everything and lose myself in the pleasure of her small hand stroking me.

"You like that, Alek?" she asks and that's when I realize I'm moaning.

"Yeah, but I'm going to have to stop you."

"You want me to stop this?" she teases, dragging her hand from my base, all the way to my crown as I bite the foil.

"No, not really, but I need to get this condom on and I might swallow it if you keep it up."

She blinks dark lashes over innocent eyes. "Distracted, are you?"

I love this playful side of her. "Wait, is this payback?" I ask. Yeah, I really took her to the edge and kept her hanging.

"For rear-ending me?"

I groan. "We really need to find a new term, because every time you say it, I want your ass."

Her eyes go wide. "I've never done that."

"I know," I say. There's so much innocence about this woman, and if I were a decent guy, I'd stay as far away as I could.

She angles her head, looking coy and demure. "There are things you don't know, Alek."

"Like what?"

"That maybe I'm saying it on purpose."

"Fuck me sideways," I say, and nearly bite my tongue. Maybe she's not so innocent after all. Or maybe I just bring this out in her.

She grins at me as I tear into the foil and go back on my knees to sheath myself. Her eyes never leave my dick as I suit up. Once done, I fall over her.

"You're a fucking tease," I say, but I'm not sure she's listening. No, her legs are going around my hips and her eyes go to half-mast.

I rub my crown over her sensitive clit, and bring her back to the boiling point before I put one hand on her face to cup her cheek as I slide inside. Fuck, she feels good. She moans as I seat myself high, and find her mouth. I kiss her deeply and move my hips, a slow, easy pace that will be torture to keep now that she's swelling around me. I push forward, and she lifts for me, taking every last inch I can give her.

"You...this...amazing," is all I'm able to get out. I slowly pull my dick out, and she claws at my back, demanding me to fuck her faster. Her wet heat wraps around me, and my balls ache for release as I pound into her, faster now, hard thrusts meant to take her over the precipice a second time.

"Alek," she cries and grabs a fistful of my hair.

"I know," I say, and boy, do I ever know. We fit together so nicely, her body so damn perfect for mine. White hot need burns through me and every muscle in my body screeches for release as we fuck. I clamp down on my teeth, wanting to prolong this—for both of us—but knowing I can't. I change the pace, and using fast blunt strokes, I slick through her wet heat. I grind my pelvis against her clit, and watch her face, wanting to see her expression when she comes all over me.

I pound impossibly deeper, stretch her more, and her mouth falls open as she lets go, her hot cum scorching my dick and balls. I gasp, trying to get air into my constricted lungs, but it's a futile effort.

"So good," she cries out, each spasm pulling at my cock, teasing an orgasm from me.

Dizzy and overwhelmed with need, I fuck her harder and faster as I chase my own climax. The next time we fuck, I'll take it slower, make it last longer. It's a promise I make to myself—one I'm not even sure I can keep. But right now, I need release and I need it now. I find her mouth again, and slide my cock into her, once, twice and when she tangles her tongue with mine, the world as I know it tilts on its axis and raw physical pleasure takes over.

Sparks shoot through my body and zap my balls, and we're both breathing hard, gasping for breath when I release inside her. I moan into her mouth, aware of her hands on my body, touching me all over like she can't get enough. I collapse on top of her, my mind a hot mess as I ride out the orgasmic bliss.

After a long moment, I inch back, cup her face in my hands, and we simply stare at each other. Probably because no words can explain what just happened here. Plus, I'm not sure it's a good idea for me to give too much power to this—whatever this really is.

I shift, and warmth moves through me as I snuggle her close. As I think about her bucket list, which led us to this bed, a small chuckle rumbles in my chest and she lifts her head to see me. My pulse jumps as I take in her tousled hair, and the sexy-as-fuck flush on her cheek.

"Something funny?" she asks.

"Bucket list number nine. Sex in a limo. I think we should talk about it."

9

ALYSSA

With my body still warm and tingling from Alek's touch, I stand at the stove, stirring tomato sauce with a huge smile on my face as Alek sits at my kitchen table reading my bucket list, his legs kicked out like he's right at home. It's weird. I barely know him, yet it feels like we've been friends for a lifetime, and I can't deny that he looks like he belongs at my table. I also can't deny that I just had the best sex of my life. The man has skills and moves I've never heard of, and after just one round, I'm addicted.

"A New York, Broadway show. I can get behind that."

"Have you ever been to one?"

"Yeah, years ago." He continues to scan the list. "A honeymoon in Jamaica, pick an avocado in Mexico." He lifts his head and looks at me. "That's a strange one."

"I know right. I also want to pick olives in Tuscany, but that's because I fell in love with the movie Under the Tuscan Sun."

"Never saw it."

"Then we must rectify that."

He rakes one hand through his hair, and my knees weaken. Even without trying the man is beyond sexy.

"Is it a chick flick?" he asks

"No, not at all," I tease. "It has car races, burning buildings, and a big explosion. You're going to love it."

He arches a mocking brow at my joke. "How could it not with a name like Under the Tuscan Sun and all."

I laugh, turn the burner off and reach for the pot of boiling pasta as he contemplates that. "I think it's your turn to tell me about your list, Alek. What are some of the things you want to do, and I don't believe sex while skydiving was on the list. You just said that to ease my embarrassment."

His smile is so sweet and warm, it moves through me and tugs at something deep and dormant. I love that he told a little white lie just to make me feel better. I'm not even sure he knows how incredibly sweet he is.

"First, I never want you to feel embarrassed with me, and second, if you're into skydiving, then sex a thousand feet above ground is definitely on my list," he says with a grin.

"Not on my list."

"I guess we could always just do it in a plane." He stands, and presses his hard chest to my back as I drain the pasta. "Need any help?" he asks, his voice rumbling through me.

"Why don't you set the table? Forks and knives are in this drawer." He pushes my hair from my neck and presses a soft kiss to my shoulder. "Mmm, that feels nice," I say. He moves away and takes his warmth with him.

"I've always wanted to surf in Hawaii," he says as he opens the drawer and pulls out the silverware.

"Oh, wow, that would be amazing."

"Do you surf?"

"Do you see any oceans around here?" I tease. "But I think it would be fun to learn." He sets the table, and grabs a pen from my counter. "What are you doing?"

"I'm adding to your list," he says scribbling something into my journal.

"You can't do that. It's *my* list, not yours."

"Too late," he says and drops the pen. "Now you get to add something to my list."

"I'll have to think on that."

I plate us up some spaghetti and meatballs and set them on the table.

"This looks delicious," Alek says. "I'm hungrier than I thought."

My stomach growls right along with his. "You only had half a sandwich for lunch and we did work up an appetite earlier."

He stirs the sauce and cuts into a meatball. "What time are we going to visit Grandma?"

I can't help but laugh as he claims my grandmother as his own. "After dinner. I'll bring her some spaghetti. Hopefully she's a bit more alert tonight. She comes and goes in and out of it." He nods like he understands. "Do you have grandparents?" I ask.

"Yeah, you'd like them. Typical grandparents. Money on my birthday, ugly socks and sweaters for Christmas."

"Do you wear them?"

"Of course, I do."

I smile at him, my heart full as I picture him in those ugly sweaters. "You must have had a wonderful childhood."

His expression changes as his gaze meets mine. He goes quiet, nodding, like he's drifting back to the past and remembering all the happy times. "I really did." Catching me by surprise, his hand slides across my small table and lightly brushes mine, lending me his strength and comfort. A need for...something wells up inside me at the tenderness in his eyes. "I wish yours was better for you."

I shrug, even though his tender touch and sweet concern

stirs my insides. "I'm okay. I had Grandma. She was awesome, Alek. She was the grandma who dressed up at Halloween, let me fill the house with friends, and did all the traditional meals at Thanksgiving and Christmas. She taught me to cook."

"I'm glad. Now I'm reaping the rewards," he says as he slurps a long strand of spaghetti.

"We were a small family of two, but Grandma filled the house with love and laughter."

"Do you want a family, Alyssa?"

"Someday, I suppose," I say. "I'm just not sure it's in the cards for me."

"Why?" he asks. "If you don't mind me prying."

"I mean, I guess I always pictured myself with a family."

"Number six on your bucket list," he reminds me.

"I'm just busy with my business and my grandmother. There's not a lot of time for anything else."

"I'm glad you made the time for me."

"Like you gave me a choice," I say, finishing it with an unladylike snort that brings a smile to his face. "You practically kidnapped me, and I think there was some bribery in there too."

"I'm like a barnacle when I set my mind to something," he teases, but the smile falls from his face when he adds, "But seriously, concussions are dangerous, and I really wanted to make sure you were okay."

My heart squeezes. "I appreciate it," I say, and as strange emotions swirl around inside my stomach, I don't want him to get the wrong idea about what I want from this, from us. "Also, there's not a lot of single guys my age around here. So, don't go flattering yourself thinking you're special," I tease, even though there is a part of me that totally believes there is something very extraordinary about this guy.

"Ah, I get it. I just happened to be the right age with the right parts."

"You nailed it."

"Yeah, I did," he says with a cute grin, and my body flushes as my pulse skitters with a new kind of want. My God, how can I want him again so quickly? Sex with him was out of this world, and I've gone without a man's touch so long, it should hold me over to the next century. But I don't want that. No, what I want is the man across from me, his inquisitive gaze locked on mine.

"Your friends, where are they all now?" he asks.

I take a sip of water as things turn deeply personal. I have no secrets, and I believe in honesty, but dredging up the past is never easy. "They went off to college and moved on to bigger towns for their careers. I'm happy for them," I say, injecting a bit of enthusiasm into my voice, but this man has proven to be astute, and I'm an easy read. Truthfully though, I am happy for my friends. I want the best for them, and it's not their fault I couldn't go. No, my abandonment issues go way back.

"You mentioned your ex was on the football team. What happened to him?"

I shake my head. "He left, like the rest of them, and he let me believe we were going to do long distance. Lying bastard," I say.

"I called it. Total douche-bag," he agrees quickly, and I grin, loving that he's quick to take my side, even though he doesn't know the circumstances. I have the feeling Alek is a ride or die kind of friend. He slams his fist into the palm of his hand. "If you want payback, just say the word."

I wave a dismissive hand. "I'm over him and he's not worth it."

"Good." He takes a bite, chews and goes thoughtful for a

while. A comfortable silence falls over us, and then he breaks it and asks, "So you never wanted to move?"

"I can't leave Grandma." I won't leave her. Sure, she has friends here, plenty of them, but she's my only relative and I'm hers. "She was always there for me, and now I'm here for her."

"I get that. I really do. But you wrote on your bucket list that you wanted to travel, see the world and live in a big city, preferably somewhere warmer than Vermont in the winter."

I roll my eyes to make light of it. "I also wrote that I wanted to have sex in a limo in New York, and I don't see that ever happening. I was a kid, Alek. Full of idyllic ideas."

"I don't know." He shrugs a broad shoulder. "I don't think you should let go of your dreams."

I stare at the man I barely know, and see the truth in what he's saying. "Tell me more about your bucket list," I say.

"I'd love to cage dive with sharks, and maybe drive a race car on a track." His eyes go big. "Oh, and maybe bull riding."

I laugh. "I'm sensing a theme here. I think you're a bit of an adrenaline junkie."

"So you've never seen the Atlantic or Pacific Ocean?" he says, glancing at my list.

"Nope, I want to put my feet in both of them."

"How about a road trip?" he says.

"In Moxie, or in your car which is still parked on Main Street."

"Good point," he says and stares at one of his meatballs like he has something on his mind. I want to ask, but close my mouth, hoping I didn't embarrass him by mentioning his broken-down car.

"Have you thought about what you're going to get Kaylee for her birthday?" I ask, changing the subject.

"No, but my buddy Jonah and his wife Quinn have a kid.

I'll give him a call. They were actually thinking about taking a drive up to visit me here."

"That will be nice."

He nods, like he's not so certain it will be.

"Sounds like you have great friends."

"I do. But like my parents, they're on my case too. Always trying to set me up and marry me off. Christ, my buddy Kane had this whole scheme to get our other friend Rider and this girl together. I was in the middle of it and didn't know."

"How could you not know it?"

"No one decided to tell me they were using me as a pawn, and I ended up punching my buddy Rider." He shakes his head and laughs. "Never mind, it's a long story."

"Did Rider and the girl end up together?"

"Yup. They're talking marriage and kids down the road. I hope they have a girl."

"Really? Why?"

"Boys are a handful," he says, like he knows a thing or two about that. I grin, thinking he and his brother must have been rowdy. "Jonah's son, Scotty, is four and nothing can slow him down. You'll see."

"I'm not so sure about that. We only agreed on five days, remember?"

"I remember," he says, and for a second I wonder if that's disappointment I hear in his voice.

"I'm sure Captain Jack will love to have a four-year-old around," I say. "Sounds like they both have the same amount of energy." I finish my last meatball and glance outside. The rain is still falling. I sigh.

"Don't like the rain?"

"I love when it rains," I say, "But it sort of interferes with my job."

He frowns. "Yeah, I guess it would, and six months of winter probably doesn't help either."

"You're right about that. I love what I do, but unfortunately, the climate here prevents me from doing it all year round." He goes quiet, like he's mulling that over, and I stand to take my dishes to the sink.

I grab a plastic container and fill it with a portion of food for my grandmother. As I do that, Alek jumps up and starts the dishes.

"You don't have to do that," I tell him.

"Oh, is there something else you'd rather I do?"

I grin at him. "Plenty of things." I hold the container up. "I have to get to the nursing home. Can I take a rain check?"

"Good thing it's raining," he says.

"If it wasn't?"

"Wouldn't matter, I'm still going to strip you naked tonight and have my way with you."

"Actually, you're not," I say, and his brow furrows. I poke him in the chest. "I'm going to strip you naked and have *my* way with you."

"Fuck," he murmurs.

"Yeah, exactly."

ALEK

Alyssa and I have been hanging out for three days now. Three fun days working together, and three fun nights falling into bed together. Come Friday, her time is up with me. Only problem is, the more time I spend around her, the more I want to extend the five-day limit. Maybe I should rear-end her again. Jesus, what am I saying and for fuck's sake I need to stop thinking about her perfect, heart-shaped ass.

As I drive us home from work—she's given up fighting me on the matter, and yes, I like taking care of her—I take in the streaks of mud on her face. It's been drizzling for the last three days, making work difficult, but we were able to finish off Mrs. Henderson's backyard. Alyssa was a little quiet as we completed the job today, and I'm pretty sure it has to do with the fact that she doesn't have any more big jobs lined up.

"I was talking to Tyler today," I say. "He called while you were talking with Mrs. Henderson."

She casts me a sideways glance. "How's his vacation going?"

"Good." I chuckle. "But he did complain about his

nagging sisters, and how they're trying to set him up with every single girl in their contact list. I'm glad it's him and not me," I say, and she smiles at me but it doesn't reach her eyes.

"How long is he gone again?" she asks.

"Three weeks."

She turns and stares out the front window. "So you're leaving then, after three weeks," she says, and that's when I realize it's not something we ever talked about.

"I might stay longer. I'm not sure. I do have to go back to Boston for Kaylee's party. Which reminds me of a couple things. One, I'd like to go to the city this weekend to get her a present, and two, my buddy Jonah texted and he and his family have decided to come up next weekend."

"Oh, that's nice," she says and looks at her hands.

"Any chance you can come to the city with me this weekend and help?" I do have to get Kaylee a present, but I have ulterior motives that I'm not about to divulge. No, she doesn't need to know what I have planned and I seriously can't wait to see her face when she finds out. "I know nothing about girls."

She grins. "I wouldn't say that."

I reach across the seat and capture her hand. "Will you come?"

"With the landscaping job complete, and just a few other contracts that aren't too big, I have some free time. We can take my truck if you want."

"I have something else in mind," I say. "Do you think your grandmother would miss you if we didn't get back in time for visiting hours?"

The freckles on her nose pinch together as she makes a face. "I think she'd be okay with that. I'll have one of her friends check in and read to her. I'll let her know tonight. She's really enjoying your visits too, you know. It's funny how she thinks she knows you."

Nope, not funny at all.

"I like visiting her too," I say, although the more time I spend with her, the more I think she *does* know who I am.

"What about Captain Jack, though?"

"Covered. Tyler told me to check in with his neighbor. They have kids and they love the dog, so they won't mind taking care of him for the night."

"For the night?"

"Yeah, I mean, they'll feed him and walk him." *Way to almost let the cat out of the bag, dude.* I never was very good at keeping secrets, yet here I am keeping a whopper of a one from her, and I fucking hate everything about that. If I tell her now will it ruin this between us? Will she end up hating me? I'm not sure that's a risk I want to take. My buddy Jamie is the risk taker, not me. As I think about him it brings a smile to my face. I'm so happy he finally found love and a home with Fallon. "I still want you to take me fishing," I say, wanting to change the subject.

"You really want to learn?" she asks, like she can't wrap her mind around that.

"Well yeah. I mean I've been spin fishing before, just never fly fishing. I'm not afraid of worms if that's what you're thinking."

She laughs at me. "We don't use worms. We bait the fish with artificial flies that's why it's called *fly* fishing."

"As long as we catch some big trout, I don't care what we use as bait. I'm looking forward to learning all your tricks and techniques, and frying those fish on the barbecue."

"It's the least I can do after you helping me with my landscaping."

"Speaking of landscaping. I mentioned your burning bush to Tyler."

She gives me the side eye like she's not sure whether this conversation has gone south or not. "Ah, okay..."

I pull into Tyler's driveway and kill the ignition. "He was all over the idea. In fact, he was hoping you could redesign his yard, front and back. He wants to hire you, and said he's been meaning to get some work done, he's just been busy."

Her mouth falls open. "Are you serious?"

"Yeah, very." I wave my hand. "This is your new playground."

With eyes as big as hockey pucks, she glances around the yard and says, "I can't believe this. The contract will go a long way in paying…"

Her voice falls off and she looks away like she's said too much. But I understand. She's responsible for her grandmother's care and bills. I don't say anything, though. I don't want to embarrass her.

"So what do you think?"

"I think I have a ton of ideas," she says, the joy back on her face. "Right over there, I think we could put some evergreens, and right there, I'd love to see rhododendrons. I can sketch it all out first."

"I'm sure that won't be necessary. But if you want, you can."

She turns back to me, her eyes so soft and so goddamn warm my heart pounds a little fast. It's insane how much I like doing things for her. Probably because she asks for nothing.

She puts her hand on mine. "You were so sweet to recommend my services, Alek."

I tap the steering wheel with my free hand. "It's possible I have ulterior motives."

"Oh," she asks, her brows lifting, a knowing gleam in her eyes.

I give a casual shrug, not wanting to scare her off, or for her to think I want more here, because I don't. Fuck, all I can hope for is that this thing between us ends amicably, and when I leave—with Alyssa never really knowing who I was—I can only hope we both have fun, and hold on to a few fond memories of this summer fling. Only problem is, it doesn't feel like my true identity is a harmless omission anymore. It feels like deception, and this is a girl who appreciates honesty. I guess I never expected this to get so complicated. Unease unfurls in my gut, and I draw in a fast breath to pull myself together.

Fuck me.

"I was thinking, maybe you might want to hang out longer, while you're working on Tyler's place."

"You want to extend the five days?" she asks, and licks her lips. My cock twitches.

"It's been kind of fun, don't you think?"

Her eyes glaze over a bit, and she tugs at her bottom lip with her teeth. Damn she's sexy.

"Oh, I think."

"So that's a yes?"

She looks around, like she's considering it. "Does Tyler really want his yard done? He really said that to you?"

"He knew who you were the second I mentioned your name." Her gaze flies back to me, and I hold my hand up. "Scout's honor."

She chuckles. "Were you really a scout?"

"No, but I ate a brownie once."

"Oh my God," she says, her laugh deep and throaty as she gets out of the truck. "I can't believe you just said that."

"What?" I say, unable to hide my smirk, as I circle the truck to meet her. "Don't you like brownies?"

"Yeah, the chocolate kind, but that's not what you're talking about." She pokes my chest, amusement dancing in her eyes. "Who was she?" she asks.

"Her name was Tori Boyd." I slide my hand around her waist, and back her up until she's pressed against the hood of her truck. I spread her legs with my knee, and settle in close.

"Sounds made up," she says, her voice a little breathless as I brush the streak of mud from her cheek. She rests her hands on my chest and splays her fingers.

I bring one hand to my mouth and kiss her fingertips, slowly, then press a soft kiss to her wrist. A quiver goes through her as she melts under my touch. "She was big into the girl scout's organization. Went all the way through the ranks," I say.

"All the way, huh?" she teases.

"She was a seventeen-year-old scout when we met. Man, you should have seen her in that uniform." I make a low whistling noise, and Alyssa shakes her head at me. "I was a seventeen-year-old asshole with one thing on his mind."

"I can just imagine." Her hands slide around my back, and she moves her hips, her sweet sex torturing my growing dick. "Actually, I don't think you've changed much over the years."

"You're not wrong, but the arrangement was mutual. I helped her get her de-flowering badge, and I—"

One hand goes up in the air to stop me. "I know what you got out of it." She rolls her eyes and feigns exasperation. "You don't have to spell it out."

"Speaking of spelling it out. That's when I learned the alphabet...with my tongue."

Dark lashes fall over lust-infused eyes. "You are so bad, but ah, yeah, I'm kind of glad you learned that."

I chuckle, loving her sexy reactions. Honestly, I have never been so comfortable with a woman, so at ease that it makes talking about anything and nothing as natural as breathing. I barely know her, yet I'm completely spellbound.

Her tongue snakes out to wet her dry lips and all I can think about is rehydrating myself with the sweetness between her legs and pleasuring her until she's screaming my name.

"What would you say if I had one of those uniforms in my closet?" she asks.

My breath stalls in my lungs and my cock rockets to life. "I'd say get back in the truck, we're going for a drive."

Her chuckle massages my balls. "It would be far too small for me now."

"Even better."

"What is it with guys and uniforms?" She rolls her eyes, but it's her grin that fucks me over. Man, I really like this girl. So strong, so independent, so fucking sweet—inside and out.

"How old were you when you lost your virginity?" I ask, and press kisses to her cheeks, nose and lips.

She sighs as I lightly brush my mouth over hers, a feathery light caress. "Seventeen, too."

"Was it with the douche?"

"Yeah, he was kind of my one and only."

I pull back. "No shit."

"Yeah."

Catching me by surprise, she goes up on her toes and presses her lips to mine for a long, affectionate kiss. Her mouth lingers as her eyes fall shut, reducing me to that hormonal seventeen-year-old again, and all thoughts of her ex evaporate from my mind. I open my mouth for her tongue and she slides it in. Desire surges through me, the only thing that matters is this woman and what she does to me.

"Mmm," she moans into my mouth. "This is much better than talking about the past, isn't it?"

I drag her closer, until her soft body is flush with mine, and run my hands down her back until I'm cupping her sweet ass, and hating the clothes that are separating us. Her nipples scrape against my chest as we practically dry hump against her vehicle.

"We could talk about all the things I'm going to do to you once I get you inside," I say.

She chuckles into my mouth. "Like feed the dog, cook dinner, and get ready to go see Grandma."

I break the kiss, and my eyes travel down the length of her as I think about the best way to get her out of her coveralls. "It's like we're an old married couple," I murmur and my heart leaps at the thought. But the funny thing is, I'm not exactly frightened by it this time.

"I never knew playing house could be so fun," she says, a fast reminder that we're not really a couple with a future.

Is that what I want?

Fuck, even if I did, once she found out that I'd been keeping my identity from her, she'd send me packing.

A car drives by and she backs up. "We'd better get inside before we get arrested for public indecency. You're leaving in a couple of weeks, but I have to live in this town."

I give her ass a slap to set her into motion, and the little squeal that follows makes me smile. "You really are an ass man, aren't you?" she teases.

"Yup, not about to deny it." She hurries ahead of me, giving an extra little shake to her backside. "What do you think you're doing?"

She glances at me over her shoulder and blinks innocently, but I know better. "Me? Nothing at all."

"Do you have any idea what it does to me when you shake your ass like that?"

Her grin is sexy and playful when she asks, "Does it make you want to help me earn my rear end-deflowering badge?"

Jesus. Fuck.

She did not just say that.

11

ALYSSA

"**N**o way!"

"You like?" Alek asks me.

I step into the three-car garage attached to Tyler's mansion, and take in the two shiny sports vehicles that look like they've never been driven. I don't know much about fancy cars, but it's easy to tell these ones are top of the line and I'm not sure I'm comfortable driving in one to the city. What if we get in a fender bender? There's a lot of elderly people in this town and getting to the highway could be hazardous.

I glance over my shoulder and find Alek watching me. "Tyler doesn't mind you using one?"

"Nope. He insisted." He presses the fob in his hand and the gray Mercedes beeps. "Hop in."

I open the door, and slide into the passenger seat, and moan as I sink into the luxurious leather. "Don't tell Moxie how much I like this," I say as I rub my hand over the dashboard. "She might disown me."

"Moxie will always be your number one." He comes around my side and crouches. The position reminds me of when we met, and how he tried to wrestle the door to my truck open. Who knew that day would lead me to his bed? "Comfortable?" he asks.

"Very, but we can take my truck. It's only an hour to the city."

"Not to the city we're going," he says, his grin mischievous, and playful and so full of anticipation I sit up a little straighter.

"What are you talking about?"

He stands without answering me. "I'll be right back," he says and closes my door before he disappears inside the house. Needing a distraction, I scroll through my phone, checking the Instagram accounts of all my friends who have moved on as I wait for him, and when he comes back, he has a duffle bag in his hand. He drops it into the trunk and jumps in beside me.

"What city are we going to?" I ask.

"There's a special toy store I need to go to."

"Where?"

He presses a button to start the vehicle and another to open the garage door. "You'll see when we get there."

"Alek," I say. "What are you up to?" I study his profile, and despite having no idea what he's up to my insides relax a bit. Over the last couple of days, he'd been acting a bit secretive, making calls on his phone, and whispering if I came into the room. I'd even seen a couple of texts from a girl named Fallon come in, but what right do I have to ask who Fallon is and what she means to him? I still don't know who she is, and I totally dislike the jealousy in my stomach, but I can't help but think all the secrecy was about this surprise trip to the city.

"Are you going to answer me?" I say, and lift my chin a little, pretending I'm upset about the whole thing when I'm secretly elated.

Still ignoring the question, he whistles innocently and

backs out of the garage. He buckles himself in, presses a button to close the garage and drives through town. We go down Main Street and when I look off into the side street, I see a vehicle in front of my grandmother's house, a young couple standing on the sidewalk admiring it.

"Take a right," I say, and Alek's gaze flashes to mine.

"What's up?"

"There's a couple looking at Grandma's place."

"You want to creep them."

"Of course I want to creep them," I say with a laugh.

He takes the turn, and we slowly drive by. I check out the license plate. "Maryland," I say. "I wonder what brings them to Bridgetown." A deep sadness goes through me, but I have no choice but to sell.

"What a gorgeous old home."

"You like it?" My mood lifts. I'm not sure why Alek liking my home fills me with a strange satisfaction.

"I love it. Drive by again?"

"No, we can go to this mystery city," I say.

He makes his way back to Main Street, and when he takes the ramp for the highway, I turn to him.

"We're not coming back tonight, are we?" I ask.

He casts me a fast glance and hits his signal light to merge into traffic. "No."

"And you're not going to tell me where we're going?"

"No."

"What about clothes?" I glance down at my jean shorts and T-shirt. "I don't have anything to wear."

"You won't need clothes," he says, and I bite back a grin at the playful way he wags his eyebrows.

I fold my arms like a belligerent child, even though I'm looking forward to finding out what he's up to, and honestly, I don't really care about our destination. I just like hanging out with Alek. Maybe a little too much.

"What if I don't want to go?" I ask.

"You do."

"Oh, do I now?" I purse my lips. "How would you know that?"

He reaches over and puts his hand on my thigh. The reassuring squeeze wraps around my heart, and as I take in his smiling face, I worry I could be in real trouble here. He's such a sweet guy, but like everyone else I know, he'll be leaving for bigger and better soon enough. An invisible hand squeezes my heart at that thought, but I paste on a smile for Alek's sake. He's pretty excited about this adventure, and I don't want to do anything to ruin it.

"You'll see. Now relax, we have a good, long drive ahead of us."

"There better be ice cream," I pout and he laughs.

"You and Kaylee would be fast friends," he says. "I always take her out for ice cream when I visit."

My heart tightens again. I love that he's so close to his family. There's no denying I want that, that I'd love to meet Kaylee and his brother and folks, and even his friends that are coming to visit, but he's not putting that offer on the table and I hate myself for even wanting that. I knew what I was getting into with him and have no one to blame but myself for these budding feelings, or that I'm a little more invested in him than I would have liked.

"Tell me more about your family," I say and sink back into the seat to enjoy the drive.

I can hear the love in his voice as he talks, and before I know it hours have gone by, and unfortunately for me, hearing his stories and the love in his heart only makes me fall a little more for him.

I watch the traffic signs go by, and hours into our drive, I have a pretty good idea where he wants to go, but I keep my mouth shut, and just enjoy this time with him.

I rest my head against the seat, lost in his voice and a long time later he says, "We're almost there."

"This must be one special toy store if you drive over six hours to reach it."

"It is," he says, as we get into the thick New York traffic. "But to be honest, this trip is more about you than it is for Kaylee."

"What do you have planned?" I ask, and my heart beats a little faster when he gives me a smile so sweet and tender, I'm not sure how I ever lived life without him.

He pulls up in front of a gigantic hotel, and puts the car into park when a valet circles the front. He stands outside the driver's side door, waiting for us to exit the vehicle.

"Ready?" Alek asks and grabs his ballcap. He puts it on and pulls it low on his forehead.

My eyes go wide, and a measure of unease worms its way through me. "Wait, what's going on? Are we staying here?" He nods, and I grasp his wrist. "Alek, this is too much."

He takes a breath and scrubs his face, his eyes leaving mine. "I want to do this, okay? I want to do this for you and the reason I didn't tell you is because I knew this is exactly how you'd react."

Tears prick my eyes. He's so incredibly sweet, so generous, but I don't need extravagant things in my life. He's a guy in between jobs and I don't want to embarrass him by pointing that out, so I simply say, "You didn't need to do this for me."

"I know. All the more reason I want to." He shifts toward me. "Aly, I want to take care of you—"

"Alek..."

"Just hear me out." I nod, and he continues with, "I know you're strong and independent—"

"Like an ant, I know," I say, wanting to lift some of the tension in my body.

He chuckles and touches my hair, running it through his

fingers. I lean into him, my breath catching at the tender way he's looking at me. "You're always taking care of everyone else, and tonight, I just want to take care of you. Say you'll let me."

"I'll let you," I say softly, my heart lodged somewhere in my throat, and he reaches over and unsnaps my seat belt, excitement in his eyes as his mood shifts.

"Come on, let's go." He pops the trunk as I open my door. I turn in time to see the big smile on the valet's face when he glances at Alek, like he knows him or something. Alek quickly hands the keys over, adjusts his cap a bit more, and pulls his bag from the trunk. He captures my hand and whisks me inside.

"Did you know that guy?"

"No," he says and inside the lobby, he glances around. We take the elevator to the registration lobby, and he guides me to a line of sofas. "I'll be right back. Wait here, okay?"

"I'm not going anywhere," I say and take in the huge lobby and all the people milling about. "I could get lost in this lobby."

Taking me by surprise, he leans down and plants a warm kiss onto my mouth. "Don't worry. I won't let you get lost, Aly."

Oh, God, it might be too late for that because I fear I already am lost—in him. I sit tight as he registers us, and less than ten minutes later, he's opening a door to the most gorgeous room, with the most amazing view over New York, that I have ever seen.

If I click my heels three time would I find myself back in small town Vermont. I'm not sure, and I'm certainly not going to chance it!

I walk closer to the window and wobble a little. "We are so high up." I turn to find him grinning at me. "I can't believe you arranged all this, and I didn't even know."

"I had a little help from a friend."

"Oh."

He tosses his bag onto the bed and unzips it. He pulls out a beautiful black dress, and holds it up.

My heart jumps and I point to it. "What's that?"

"Looks like a dress to me," he teases. "You didn't bump your head again, did you?"

"Not funny. Why do you have a dress?" I eye him. "Are you trying to tell me something?"

He laughs. "I didn't bring you all the way to New York to tell you I'm a cross-dresser. Not that there's anything wrong with that. Each to his own, right? But I brought you here to see a Broadway show and go for a limo drive."

I sink onto the sofa near the window, my legs no longer able to hold me upright. My pulse skitters, and my throat grows so tight it's hard to talk. "Alek..." is all I'm able to say, as my eyes water. "I can't believe this."

"I'm full of surprises today, huh?"

"Yeah, you're full of something," I say, and when he angles his head, a note of confusion on his face, I add, "I mean that in the nicest way possible."

"Of course. What else could it have possibly meant?" he says and holds his hand out to me.

A hurricane of need sweeps through me as I cross the room and frame his face with my hands. I go up on my toes and brush my lips over his. "How? When?" I ask, my words deep and raspy as emotions clog my throat.

"Like I said, I had a little help from a friend. My buddy Jamie's wife Fallon helped me put this all together. She's a nurse. You'd really like her."

She sounds like someone I'd like to meet, but I don't say that. Alek and I aren't in this for the long term. We're not in a relationship where we introduce each other to friends and family, although he knows Grandma. Not that I had a choice in the matter. No, sweet Alek insisted on driving, and continues to insist on taking care of me. Yes, I'm an independent woman, but I have to say I like it when he does.

I like him.

"You lied to me," I say, and slowly lift my gaze to his.

His head inches back a bit. His muscles tense, and his teeth clench with an audible click. Truthfully, I'm a bit surprised by his reaction.

"What are you talking about?" he asks, and his throat makes a gurgling sound as he swallows.

"You said I wouldn't need clothes."

He relaxes, his shoulders dropping. "Oh right."

"What did you think I meant?"

"I...nothing. I didn't know what you meant," he says. "Want to try this on?"

"How did you know my size?"

His grin turns sexy, playful. "I had my hands and mouth all over you numerous times, remember."

"Oh, I remember," I say. Never in my life would I forget that. I take the dress from him. I glance at my sandals. "Please tell me you have shoes in there."

"Size seven, right?"

"I won't ask how you know." He hands them to me, and something niggles loose in my brain. "Wait, did you say a limo ride?"

"Yeah, I want to start checking things off your bucket list."

This is all too much, too expensive. I put my hand on his chest and his strong heartbeat pulses beneath my palm. "Alek, you didn't—"

"I wanted to." He checks his watch. "You better hurry. We have dinner, a show and then a drive around town."

He slaps my ass and I squeal with eagerness. "I need to

shower and freshen up. It was a long ride." I glance at his bag. "Did you pack me any makeup or underwear?"

"You don't need makeup," he says and puts his hand on my cheek. His eyes are infused with warmth and tenderness when he adds, "You're beautiful without it."

A bone deep warmth moves through me, at the sweet way he's looking at me, like I'm the only one in the world that matters to him. God, I could be in real trouble here. I work to sound normal when I ask, "What about underwear?"

His teasing grin returns. "They'll just be in my way later."

I shake my head at him as waves of excitement roll through me. I take a step toward the bathroom, stop and turn around. "You know, you should have told me what you were up to."

He scrubs his chin, his eyes serious. "You wouldn't have let me."

"Maybe..." I cock my head. "Or maybe I would have packed my too-tight girl scout uniform."

"Jesus. Fuck."

12

ALYSSA

The warm night air curls around us as we exit the theater and walk through Times Square. To think that yesterday I was on my hands and knees digging in the dirt and today I'm all dressed up and just watched a Broadway show. I'm living in a fantasy world, I get that, but I don't care anymore. I'm just going to enjoy Alek and the little time we have together. When it's all over, I'll lick my wounds in solitude. Until then, I'm all in, game for anything and everything.

Anticipation dances in the air as Alek puts his arm around me and tugs me close. I revel in the strength of his hand on my body as we stroll through the crowded streets, which are so very different from home. There isn't one familiar face in this city, and I'm sort of enjoying the anonymity of it. No one knows my business and I don't know theirs. Knowing I'll never set eyes on these people again is a bit freeing.

The energy in the crowd buzzes around me, and I feed off it. I lift my chin and smile up at the incredibly kind and generous man who set this all up for me. He dips his head, and need wells up inside me when he smiles. I'm going to have a lot of healing to do, it's true, but how can a girl not fall for a guy like him?

Earlier this evening, after showering and dressing, I exited the bathroom to find Alek dressed in a suit that showcased his broad shoulders and athletic body. The man cleans up nice, and while he looked amazing in the suit, it was all I could do not to tear it off his body and make love to him on the king-sized bed. But he had dinner plans and tickets for the show, and now...well, now we're going for a limo ride, and I can hardly believe I'm going to check that off my bucket list. Equal amounts of nervousness and excitement invade my belly, and a strange giggle climbs out of my throat.

Pleasure smolders in his eyes when they meet mine. "Having fun?" he asks as he tugs me closer, and drops a kiss onto the top of my head. My heart squeezes, my body so consumed with need for this man it's a bit overwhelming.

"I am," I say and melt into him as he guides me through the streets. Someone bumps into me as they walk by fast. "It's a good thing I have you, Alek. I'd get lost out here."

"You've got me," he says, and I fight back the emotions beating my chest like a gorilla's fists, warning of danger. The truth is, while I've got him tonight, there is no future. I'll have to move on without him, but how can I ever think about being with another guy after our time together. It's unnerving and—

Stop!

Okay, I am not going to think beyond tonight. I am only going to enjoy the now.

After giving myself a quick lecture, I take a deep breath, let it out slowly, and let Alek guide me around the corner.

"Oh, we're right here," I say, surprised when I see the hotel.

He laughs and talks to the valet. A few minutes later, our limo arrives and the driver jumps out to open the back door for us. I'm about to slide in, but stop and put my mouth to Alek's ear.

"I'm glad this was never checked off my list, because there's no one else I'd rather take this ride with," I say.

"Good," he says his voice thick and husky, full of desire.

I slide into the seat, and stretch my legs out in comfort. My dress rises on my thighs, and I tug on it. I'm not wearing any panties, and there's no need to flash our driver. Seriously though, this is all so out of character for me and I have to say, I love it. Alek speaks to the driver and a few minutes later, we're cruising through the streets, Alek, seated beside me, his hard thigh warm and strong, pressed against mine.

He takes my hand and brings it to his mouth. My blood pumps faster, a surge of need racing through me. The divider between the front and back goes up and my nerve endings tingle.

"Do you think he can hear us?" I ask, as Alek puts a hand on my bare thigh.

"No." His gaze moves over my face. "Do you have any idea how hard tonight was for me?"

My pulse spikes. Did he not enjoy the show? "What?"

He takes my hand and puts it on his erection. "Oh," I say and giggle, like a silly schoolgirl.

"Yeah, oh. Seeing you in this dress, and knowing I was the guy who got to take it off you tonight...Jesus." He scrubs his face. "I could hardly watch the show."

"You did seem a bit distracted," I say.

He shifts in his seat, and puts his face near my ear. He breathes me in as he whispers, "All I could think about was putting my cock in you."

"Me too," I say, my voice a breathless whisper. His hand slides up my thigh.

"Knowing you have nothing on under this is a total mind-fuck." His fingers inch higher, and I widen my thighs to accommodate him. He growls at the invitation, and lightly strokes my swelling clit.

"Wet, just the way I like you," he says, and teases my cleft, circling it until my chest is rising and falling and I'm pressing my head into the back rest. That's when I notice the sunroof. I stare up at the stars as the man I'm falling for works his strong fingers between my thighs, always putting my needs before his own. I realize this is all about me, but I want to do something more for him.

"Alek," I murmur.

"Yeah?"

"This is my bucket list fantasy, right?"

He slides his thumb over my clit, and my hips lift. "Yeah, baby, this is all about you."

Honest to God, I've never felt so sexy, so wanted in my entire life. A girl could get used to this kind of attention.

"Then I need you to do something for me," I say.

"I'll do whatever you want. All you have to do is ask."

If I asked him to stay in Bridgetown, would he?

I quickly squash that thought.

Don't go there, Alyssa.

"Look up." His gaze follows mine to the sunroof. "I want you to stand, and look outside."

"Yeah, you want that?" he asks, his fingers still working magic between my legs.

"I want that."

He moves his fingers and I groan. "You sure you want me to stop?" he asks, his voice husky, his eyes half-mast with desire.

"Well no, but yes."

He chuckles and hits a button to open the sunroof. A warm breeze blows inside as he stands and pokes his head out. He looks back inside. "It's gorgeous out here. Want to come up?"

"I'm interested in something else that's up," I tell him, and reach for his zipper.

"Aly," he murmurs, sounding tortured and aroused at the same time. "What are you doing?"

I shift on the seat and my mouth parts, hungry to taste him as I free him from his pants.

"It's what I want," I say, meaning every word of it. Pleasuring him brings me a tremendous amount of pleasure. "It's part of my bucket list fantasy. Well, it is now, because it's you I'm with. Now look at the stars and hang on for the ride."

He curses as he puts his head back out, and I grin, loving that I can tease, arouse and please him like this. With his pants still around his hips, I breathe in his heady scent and weigh his big, gorgeous cock in my hand before tugging him from base to tip. He swells, his veins filling with heated blood. I can't hear him, or see him but the way his cock is twitching and pulsing tells me everything I need to know. He loves this as much as I do.

I inch forward to take him into my mouth, but no way can I take all of him. That's okay, my hand can do the rest. I move my head back and forth, and tug his pants a bit lower so I can massage his balls. His hips jerk forward, and I like that he can't see what I'm doing. He can only feel.

Pre-cum spills from his slit, and I lap at the tanginess. I swirl my tongue around his crown and drink him all in. He moves his body, pumping into my mouth and I let him work his cock, keeping my lips wrapped around him so he can fuck me.

His head dips. "I'm close, babe," he says. "So fucking close."

In typical Alek fashion, he tries to pull back, but I put my arms around his body to prevent him from breaking away. I want his cum. Every single drop of it. When he gets the gist, his growls reach my ears, and I take him deeper, until he's in my throat. He pounds on the roof and I grin inwardly.

That's it, Alek, let go for me.

His hips move faster as his orgasm mounts, his cock so hard now, so full of blood, I'm sure he's not even thinking straight. I suck until hollows form in my cheeks, and race my hand up and down his shaft. He reaches inside the vehicle, and fists my hair. For a second I think he's going to pull me off, but his hand starts following the motion of my head.

My own body pulses with need, and since I'm currently wearing no panties, my naked thighs are sopping wet with desire. Alek is really going to like that. The thought brings a smile to my face. I like making him happy and honest to God, everything I do with this man feels so good. So right. And that's scary.

His entire body stiffens, and a second later, he fills my mouth with his tangy cum, his muscles trembling with his climax. I moan in sheer bliss as I take it all in. But he keeps coming and coming, his hard cock bursting with pleasure. I can't swallow fast enough. Some drips down my chin, and I have no idea why, but it turns me on even more. I lick him clean and lightly rub his balls, a gentle caress to milk every last drop from him. I inch back, and his gorgeous cock slides from my mouth. Alek drops down into the seat across from me. He's windblown and breathless, his eyes half-lidded and sated. Desire seeps under my skin and my sex clenches.

"Aly," he whispers, and goes down on his knees. He brushes his thumb over my face, cleaning me. "Aly, babe. God damn you're incredible. This pretty mouth of yours took me so fucking deep." He presses hot, open-mouthed kisses to my eyes, my nose, and lips, as his hands slide up my damp thighs.

"So wet and needy for me," he growls. "I need to lick your soaked little pussy, Aly. I need my mouth on you."

Before I realize what's happening, his hands are on my

hips and he's lifting me until I'm the one looking through the sunroof. Wind whips my hair as I lift my gaze to the starry night, but I can't think about the beauty of the night sky right now, not when Alek is pushing my dress to my waist, and kissing a hot path to my sex.

His wet mouth closes over me, sucks on me as he parts my damp lips with the soft blade of his tongue. "So good," I cry out and grip the roof to hang on. This wasn't really what I had in mind when I wrote sex in a limo in my journal. No, this is a million times better. Everything with Alek is better.

He swirls that talented tongue of his until I'm rocking into his ravenous mouth. Hard flicks over my clit steals the air from my lungs, and he inches two fingers into my tight core.

"God, yes," I murmur, my legs growing weak, but he holds my body, always there to lend a hand—or a tongue—when I'm about to fall. That's when it occurs to me that I trust him, and I haven't trusted in a very long time.

His tongue rolls over me, slow leisurely licks that turn into harder laps as I moan and writhe and move up and down to fuck his fingers. One hand moves to my backside, and my heart seizes. I've never done that, but for the first time in my life I want a man to touch me there, but only because that man is Alek. I want to try everything with him, despite the fact that it's going to be emotional suicide.

His finger circles my tight opening, gently presses into me, and I relax to grant him entrance. His growl of pleasure reaches my ears, and never taking his mouth from my clit, he slides the two fingers in my sex in and out, in and out, creating a delicious friction. My muscles quiver around him, and he pushes his pinkie a little deeper into my backside. The triple delight is more than I can take.

I'm dizzy, giddy, completely lost in what he's doing to me. Mr. Right in my nightstand will never hold up after this night. He works his pinkie in more, stretching me. Sensations sizzling through my body. I've never felt so full before, so completely pleasured.

My muscles tighten, every nerve ending firing as he works those deft fingers inside me. I'm so close, but I don't want this moment to end. I try to pull back, but he's relentless, holding me to his mouth, intent on pulling an orgasm from me.

He sucks my clit and I groan at the intense pleasure centered on my core. I gasp for breath, can't seem to fill my lungs. He nibbles on my clit, a vicious tease, and circles the sensitive bundle of nerves inside me. He certainly knows how to touch me just right to tease and prolong the pleasure, placing me right at the cliff's edge, where he leaves me hovering on the brink of ecstasy.

I love every second of it.

I come. Hard. An intense explosion that shuts down my brain. The world closes in on me, and the stars I'm seeing are behind my eyelids are not in the night sky. I call out his name, over and over, but it gets carried away in the wind. My God, sex with this man just keeps getting better and better. He slowly pulls his fingers out, and circles my clit, pressing slow tender kisses to my nether lips as he brings me back to earth.

My body stops shaking and his strong hands grip my hips and pull me back inside. My gaze locks on his and neither of us speak. We look at each other for a long time, and I have to say I have never felt closer to anyone in my entire life.

"Come here," he whispers, and puts his hand around my head to bring my mouth to his. His kiss is softer, a little more mellow, less urgent, but just as profound as earlier. A tremble goes through me as my heart beats faster.

"Alek, every inch of my body...I can't even explain it. But I'm tingling all over." He gazes at me, the intensity on his face is like an aphrodisiac and I begin to heat up again.

"I guess that's one thing I can cross off my list."

His smirk is delicious as he leans closer, puts his mouth to my ear.

"You can't cross it off yet, Aly. We're far from finished." He cups my breasts through my dress, and a moan rumbles in his throat. "You see, I haven't spent enough time here and that's a fucking tragedy, don't you think?"

I moan as he pinches my hard nipples. "Yeah, I think."

"A re you paying attention?" Alyssa asks, her forehead creasing as she frowns at me.

I laugh and hold my hands up. "Absolutely. You have my undivided attention," I tell her as she showcases the different types of flies and tells me how and when they're used.

She spent the last thirty minutes teaching me how to rig my pole and now I know everything about floating lines, leader lines, loop knots, tippets and rings. It's fascinating how much she knows. Her depth of knowledge and passion fills my soul with warmth and admiration.

"You don't seem to be listening."

"I am," I say, but I know where she's coming from. I can't seem to drag my attention from her face, and the sheer pleasure in her eyes as she rigged the rod with speed and skill. I've never seen such focus, or experience such an easy intimacy with any woman.

"Okay, then what is this?" she asks and holds a fly up for me to identify.

"That, my sweet Alyssa, is called Pat's Rubberlegs."

"And this?"

"That one's easy." I take it from her. "It's a nymph, like you."

She arches a brow. "You think I'm a mythical female spirit?"

I drop a kiss onto her cheek. "You're definitely mythical, Aly. I've never met anyone quite like you before." She gives me the sweetest smile and my mind goes back to the fun we had in New York last weekend. After our limo ride, we went back to the hotel and made love until the wee hours of the morning. Then we spent the day shopping and picking up a gift for my niece. Only problem is the more time I spend with this woman, the harder and harder it's going to be to leave. But I have a hockey career to think about, and her life is here in Vermont.

"Are you ready to learn how to read the water?"

"Teach me."

I glance down at the camouflage waders I'm wearing. They were her grandfather's, and she kept them in her storage shed, unable to part with them. She's in a pair of tan-colored ones, and she shouldn't look sexy, but my God, she does. With her hair tied back in a ponytail, the freckles on her nose darkening in the summer sun, a face free of makeup, and a big smile on her face, she's totally in her element, and has never looked more adorable.

"Something funny?" she asks as she follows my gaze down to her waders. "I mean, I know these waders aren't my girl scout outfit and—"

"You are beautiful, Alyssa. I've got a boner just looking at you."

She rolls her eyes in disbelief. "Yeah right."

I take her hand and put it over my crotch.

She laughs. "Oh my God. You're still that horny seventeen-year-old, Alek. What am I going to do with you?"

I put my hand around her fishing rod. "Maybe later you can rig another pole."

"You are so bad," she says. "Now come on, let's get in the water, maybe that will help cool you down. If not, be careful. We don't want the fish nipping at the wrong...pole."

"Funny girl."

I rein in my lust for the time being, and step beside her, as she glances out over the rushing water. I study her face, take in her concentration and it generates a new kind of warmth and need inside me. I love this side of her. Actually, I love all sides of her.

Careful, dude. This is a summer fling.

What if I want more?

"We call that flat," she says as she points to a pool of unmoving water. "That's where fish go to rest, and you'll rarely get a bite there. Can you show me another flat?" she asks, testing me to see if I'm paying attention, no doubt.

"Right there," I say and point to an area further down.

"You're a fast learner," she says, and I puff my chest up at the compliment.

"I'm good at a lot of things."

She shakes the rod in my hand. "Get your mind on the rod, Alek."

"Oh, it is," I say and she laughs. The sweet sound curls around me.

"See how the water rushes over those rocks. That's called the riffle and that's where we're going to catch our fish." She points. "Look around those medium to small boulders. See how it builds a foam line? The front is a great place to catch a fish and so is the back of a boulder where fish can be resting as insects tumble by. We want to make sure our fly drifts naturally into that foam. Watch me."

She throws her line out a couple of times and hits her mark. Her fly drifts down, and she pulls it back in. "You want to try." I nod and she steps behind me, to help guide the movement. I don't get it the first few times.

"You need to mend the line to push it upstream and allow the fly to drift naturally through the current. If fish see an unnatural drift, they will not eat your presentation." She takes it from me and shows me how to do it.

"You make it look so easy."

"It takes practice. It took me years to master it." I try again. "That's it, you're getting there."

"Nice," I say as my fly drifts down the stream. Alyssa grabs her rod and picks a different spot.

We spend a few minutes in silence, the warm sun shining down on us and I have to say, I haven't relaxed like this in a long time.

"You must have spent a lot of time with your grandfather."

She nods. "Every Sunday afternoon, actually. Until he became ill."

"I'm sorry. What happened?"

"Lung cancer." She shakes her head. "He loved his cigars." A beat of silence and then, "You would have liked him, Alek."

"I bet I would have. Were Rose and Vince your mother's or father's parents?"

I pull my line in and cast it again. I stare at my fly as it glides toward the foamy water.

"You're getting it, Alek," she says.

"That's because you're a good teacher."

Her attention slides back to her fly. I take in her profile, the look of longing on her face. I'm not sure she's going to answer my question, but after a long silent minute she says, "They're my father's parents."

I don't want to open old wounds, but I have an overwhelming urge to know more—everything—about this kind and giving woman, so I carefully ask, "What...happened to your parents?"

A rush of air leaves her mouth, and unease invades my gut as another minute of silence stretches on. "Dad was in the military. He met Mom when he was stationed in Fort Bragg, North Carolina."

"Army," I say quietly and she nods. "What about your mother's parents, did you know them?"

"My mother lost her parents in a car accident when she was in her twenties. I was born while my father was overseas actually, and when he came back he wasn't the same, or so I was told. My crying was a trigger for him, and he started drinking heavily, drugs. You name it. He basically told my mother if I didn't go, he would. I was dropped off with his parents." A humorless laugh tumbles out of her throat. "She made her choice."

Anger flares hot inside me as I take in the torment on her face. Jesus, the thoughts of her just getting tossed away breaks my fucking heart. I shake my head, my fingers curling and uncurling, wanting to pull her to me and keep her safe for the rest of her life. She's a survivor, can take care of herself, but that doesn't mean I don't want to be there for her—be the guy she can really count on.

"I don't know where she is or where he is or even if they're together." She shrugs, nonchalantly but it contradicts the haunted expression in her eyes. Fuck, all I want to do is drag her in my arms and make everything better. "They disappeared, never to be heard from again."

"Did you ever want to go look for them?" I ask, even though I want to say more, like how the fuck can a mother just abandon her child and why the hell didn't they all get the help they needed?

"No." Her head drops and she stares into the rushing

water. "Why would I chase down people who didn't want me?"

My blood runs cold as her words tear at my heart. "Yeah," I say quietly, keeping my emotions contained because an outburst is not what she needs from me, but the need to protect her is growing stronger by the second. "Sounds like your Dad wasn't well."

"No, he wasn't, and I don't know whether he didn't want help, or couldn't get help." She casts me a quick glance. "I don't talk about this, Alek. Ever. I'm not really sure why I am right now."

She trusts me. That's why she's telling me. It's a goddamn honor that she chose me to share something so painful and private with, and I'm a goddamn idiot for not being straight up with her from the beginning.

"Your secrets are safe with me, Aly." I draw a breath to steady myself, and try to quiet my racing heart before I say, "I'm glad you had Rose and Vince." A warm smile touches her mouth.

"Me too, but it wasn't easy for them either, not knowing what happened to their son. But they gave me the best life they could." She puts her hand over her heart. "They filled me up with love."

"You deserve all the love, Aly," I say quietly, as everything I feel for her rushes over my skin like a windstorm. Our eyes meet, lock together, as my heart hurts for the little girl who'd been abandoned. "I can see why you won't leave here." She spent a lifetime of everyone leaving her—her parents, friends, boyfriend—but sweet Aly, well, she's full of integrity and character, and doesn't have a mean bone in her body. No way will she hurt those she loves the way she'd been hurt.

"I'm not leaving," she says matter of factly, emotions flickering in her eyes.

No, she's not, but I am. Fuck, I'm no different than

anyone else in her life. I lift my head to find her looking at me.

"I'm okay, Alek."

"I know," I say.

"I don't want you to get the wrong idea here."

I angle my head, not sure where she's going with this. "About what?"

"Us. What's between us is just a fling. A fun summer adventure. I'm not looking for anything that resembles a relationship. I know you're passing through, and I'm okay with that. What we have here," she says, her voice so sure and steady, my muscles tense and my heart retreats. "It's all I want."

I swallow past a tight throat, and struggle to ignore the heavy ache in my chest. "Yeah, me too," I say, at the sobering reminder of what this is and what it isn't.

Shit, I have a hockey career to get back to, and she has a grandmother to take care of. It's not like I've been thinking about a future together, or wondering if we could somehow make it work. I scoff. Shit, I'm not about to ask her if we could figure out a way to make it work.

Not now anyway.

"I got one," she says, her eyes wide as she refocuses on fishing. I stand back, work to ignore the lump in my stomach as I watch in speechless fascination as she pulls the line, the fish fighting the whole way. "Can you grab me the net?"

I trudge through the water and come back with the net for her, and she scoops the fish up.

"What a beauty," she says and holds the net out for me to see a good twelve-inch speckled trout.

I rub my stomach. "Good eating tonight."

"I thought we were doing catch and release," she teases and pretends she's going to release him back into the water.

"Oh, hell no," I say and take the net from her.

"Want me to teach you how to clean it?"

"Nope, I know how." I take the fish to the shore, and grab the knife from her tackle box. I make quick work of cleaning it, and don't hear her coming up behind me. Her fingers brush over my hair, and I glance at her, note the sudden shift in her mood. Her fingers move to my face, and she leans into me, like she needs the connection. Her heat reaches out to me, and eyes that are soft, full of desire meet mine. As I soak in her warmth, I take a breath, and stand. My mouth finds hers, and a shudder races through her.

"Do you think that's enough for dinner?" she asks and gestures toward the fish. "Or do you want to stay longer, until you catch one." She steps closer until her body is flush with mine.

"If I'd known fly fishing turned you on, I would have asked you to take me here earlier."

She chuckles. "That's not what's turning me on." She puts her hand over my heart and it beats rapidly against her palm. "I thought we'd go home, and get naked and I could be your catch of the day."

I drop everything. "You don't have to ask me twice."

ALYSSA

As Alek negotiates my truck though the downtown core, my gaze wanders to his big hands, hands that have touched me all over with passion and care, and are soon going to be on my body again, inside and out. Warmth threads through me, shimmering over all my erogenous zones.

He casts me a glance, and I grin, sensing the anticipation in him. I have to say, I loved fishing with him this afternoon. I loved teaching him all the tricks, and I loved the enthusiasm, strength and confidence that poured from his every pore, as he followed my careful instructions. He's athletic and energetic, a real natural at everything he does. But what I loved the most about fishing with him was the way his steady eyes stared at me, taking pleasure in the mere sight of me enjoying my favorite pastime—at least, it used to be my favorite until I met Alek.

And therein lies the problem. Being with him, talking, touching, or just hanging out, has quickly become my favorite thing to do. Which is why I straight up told him that I didn't want more. It was a lie, yes, a big, fat bold-faced lie to be exact, but after talking about my past, I didn't want him to think he was following in the footsteps of the people who came and went from my life, disappearing without so much as a backward glance.

We both knew what we were getting into here. He told me he was only here for a short time, and no way do I want him to feel any sort of obligation to me because we've been spending every possible moment together, enjoying one another, and having out-of-this-world sex. I just want us to both see, and appreciate this for what it is—and for what it isn't. My broken heart is my responsibility, not his.

"You're quiet," he says softly, and reaches across the cab and takes my hand.

"Just sleepy," I say. Why wouldn't I be? We've been falling into bed together every night, lost in each other for hours, but I wouldn't change a thing, even if his impending absence is going to gut me in much the same manner he gutted that fish.

"Thanks again for teaching me how to fly fish," he says. "That was fun, and I think I was getting the hang of it."

"We can do it again," I say. "Practice makes perfect." My heart quivers in my chest as I take in his strong profile. "Maybe you can teach me to play hockey." His brow instantly furrows, and he tugs at the collar of his T-shirt, like it's suddenly choking him. "You did say that was what you liked to do, right?"

"Yeah, sure," he says. "That's something we could do."

"I once read an article that says sharing hobbies makes relationships hotter. Not that we're in a relationship, and not that things between us could get hotter," I add with a small laugh. "But you know what I mean." As the muscles on his jaw ripple, I ask, "What position do you like?"

His eyes briefly close and for a second it seems like he's at war with himself, but then his gaze slides to mine and he gives a wicked grin when he says, "I like all positions."

A surge of pleasure shoots through me as my mind drifts back, recalling every moment in that limo last weekend. God, the way that man touched me. The way I touched him. It was so risky, so out of character for me. So much fun.

"One track mind much?" I ask, but who am I to talk.

We pull into Tyler's driveway and I stretch my arms out before opening my door. I slide from the vehicle and Alek is right there, collecting the cooler and taking my hand in his. Inside the house, Captain Jack comes barreling down the hall looking for food and love.

"I better take him out, and fill his bowl," Alek says as I bend to pet the dog. Captain Jack begins to sniff my pants, dancing around me in a frenzy.

"You smell the fish on me, Jack?" I ask. Jack barks, and jumps up and down like he's jacked up on Red Bull. "The scents are obviously driving him crazy." I crinkle my nose. "I better go jump in the shower." I lean in, press my lips to Alek's, and give him a look full of intimacy and promise when I say, "See you soon."

"Sooner than you think," he says, and ushers Jack outside. "Make this a quick one buddy."

Chuckling, I kick off my shoes and make my way upstairs. I strip off in the master bathroom, since I pretty much moved in here after the first time we had sex, and turn the spray on to hot. Steam fills the room, and I take a peek at myself in the fogging mirror. My freckles have darkened, and the smudges under my eyes remind me that I haven't been getting a great deal of sleep. I'm not complaining. The well-fucked woman look suits me. I grin at that, and push my mess of hair from my face, and step into the gigantic, open concept shower with dials I've yet to figure out, and stand under the spray. A low moan catches in my throat as I revel in the warmth.

"I could hear your moans in the hallway. You better not have started without me," Alek teases, and my heart jumps. My God, his voice alone does the craziest things to me. I wipe the glass, and need tugs low in my pelvis as I devour the sight of him as he strips his clothes off. He's so goddamn perfect it leaves me breathless. My gaze drops to take in the hardness in his cock and I know it, the second he touches me I'm going to fall apart, in so many ways.

He slides in behind me, and I glance over my shoulder as he tugs me against his body. Damn, it's so nice to be held by him. My eyes drift shut as I lay my head against his chest and listen to the beating of his powerful heart. Right there, that's his need reaching out to me, a need that matches my own. I exhale a shallow breath as my mind drifts, branching off in erotic directions.

His fingers slide over my naked skin, a barely there caress as he outlines my curves and there's no denying that I could so get used to this. It's scary, really. Scary how much I like this guy, how much fun we're having, how this all feels so...right.

"I missed you," he whispers, breathing the words into my hair.

"You were only gone five minutes."

"Five minutes too long." He spins me around and I nearly gasp at the dark intensity—the possession—in his eyes as his mouth closes over mine. Tension builds in my body as he kisses me deeply, hungrily, like a man hell bent on making up for being deprived of what he wanted.

His tongue finds mine, tangles playfully, relentlessly, and need washes over me. He growls into my mouth, and my nipples harden and press against his chest. His hand slides up my back, and he grabs a fistful of hair and gives a little tug.

My God, I love this rough, demanding side of him. I nearly come from the sheer need in his eyes.

His mouth moves to my neck, his lips like fire on my skin, and I moan as he lightly sinks his teeth into my sensitive flesh, like he's marking me as his. I reach out, and take his hard cock into my hands, giving it a few long strokes.

"Is this what you plan on using to bait your catch of the day?" I tease.

"Yes, and to prepare for my feast, I plan to tie you up and take my time devouring every inch of you."

My sex flushes hot and he reaches down and slides a thick finger into me. I rock against him, wanting more, wanting...everything.

He scoops up the bar of soap, manly soap that smells like a mixture of pine and cedarwood. I love that I'm going to smell like him all night. He lathers my body, leaving heat and need everywhere he touches, and I close my eyes, welcoming the delicious sensations. With my skin soaped from my neck to my toes, he pumps shampoo into his hands, and washes my hair. As he touches me like I'm some sort of treasure, a new kind of closeness fills my soul.

"So nice," I say, a soft moan tumbling out of my mouth.

"You like this, Aly? You like me taking care of you like this?"

"Yes." I answer him honestly. No sense denying that I like handing myself over to him.

"Good, because once I rinse you off, I plan on taking care of you, every damn inch of you," he says, his hand sliding down my body and cupping my ass. My pulse leaps in my throat. Is he talking about—

"This virgin ass. It's mine," he whispers into my ear. Heat floods my sex, and he adds, "I want all of you. Tell me I can have it."

"You...you can have it," I say as he backs up and puts me

directly under the rain shower nozzle. Hot water pours over my body and I tilt my head to rinse away the shampoo. The enticing scent of soap reaches my nostrils as Alek washes his own body. I run my hands over my breasts, and down my stomach, cleansing the last remnants of the soap from my skin.

As hot water drips between my spread legs, my sex aches for him and deciding to relieve some of the pressure I put my hand between my thighs and lightly touch myself. I exhale a soft mewling sound and grin when his heated curses reach my ears. Under the guise of touching myself deeper, I bend forward a bit and brush my ass over his steel rod, taunting him.

"Fucking tease," he says and gives my ass a slap. I gasp, but it's from utter pleasure. "Oh, you like that, do you?"

He presses his chest to my back, and slides one hand around me to cup my breast, and his hand slides lower. His finger joins mine inside my body and I can't believe how deliciously dirty, how incredibly arousing it is to have both of our fingers inside me at the same time.

"Yeah, that's it, Aly. Show me how you fuck your fingers when you're in bed alone." I work my finger in my sex faster, and with his big hand swallowing mine, he pushes against my wrist, moving it back and forth over my clit. "Let's get this hot little cunt all ready for my big cock."

"Oh, my God," I gasp out, his filthy words stoking the fire inside me and doing insane things to my pussy.

My muscles lightly clench around our fingers, and he chuckles into my ear. "Your sweet cunt and ass are mine tonight, babe. I'm going to bury my face between your legs and eat you until you're so goddamn delirious, you'll be begging me to put my cock in your sweet pussy and tight ass."

"Alek," I gasp as intense pleasure ripples between my legs, and I rock my hips, taking both our fingers to the third knuckle, yet unable to get him deep enough. He moves his body and bends until his hard cock is pressed against my ass cheeks. He rubs himself against me, and an intense pleasure hits so hard, there's no stopping it now. Wet heat gushes from my sex, and his growl wraps around me and feeds the desire coursing through my veins. I clench hard, my chest rising and falling rapidly as I gasp for breath, lost in him, and unable to think about anything other than the intense explosion between my legs. I clutch air, searching for something to hold on to. Alek's arm goes around my waist, anchoring me to him, keeping me safe and steady.

He drags his finger from my body, and runs it up my belly to my nipple, swirling my hot juices over my engorged bud. His breath is hot as he exhales against my earlobe and says, "I love making you come." He spins me around, dipping his head to taste my nipple with the soft blade of his tongue. Emotions and sensations ripple through me as he slowly, leisurely, sweeps it over my hard bud and one thought dances around in my brain. Why did I ever think he was the kind of guy I could have a brief hook-up with?

He turns the spray off and wraps me in a big fluffy towel before tying one around his waist. A second later, I'm splayed on the bed, and that's when I notice the neckties laid out. My heart leaps. He was serious when he said he was going to tie me up.

He grins at me, and with a flick unties the towel at his waist. It falls to the floor. "You have something to say, Aly?" His tongue snakes out and he swipes it over his bottom lip as I splay my arms and legs, giving him the answer he's looking for.

"You hooked me in, now I'm yours to do what you want with."

"There's a lot I want to do."

"Why don't you show me," I say, and I gesture to the

necktie. His grin turns wicked as he snatches up the tie and wraps it around his hand as he circles the bed, like a predator toying with its prey. I'm pretty sure I've never been this turned on in my entire freaking life. He touches my knee, trails his finger up my inner thigh, and parts my lips. He angles his head to see my sex.

"So fucking pretty," he says. One thick finger slides inside me, and my hips lift. "I'm going to wreck this sweet pussy tonight," he says, his intense gaze sliding to mine.

"Yes," is all I can manage to say.

His expression changes, softens, as his hand slides lower to tease my back passage. "But don't be afraid. When I take you here, I'm going to make it good for you. I promise."

Every inch of my skin burns with want for this man. "I trust you," I say, and for one brief second, something darkens his expression.

"I'd never purposely hurt you, Aly," he says, quietly.

"I know," I tell him and move my hips up and down, forcing his finger inside me deeper. His expression changes, and his grin is devilish as he removes his finger, so goddamn agonizingly slow it hits all my hot spots, and I almost come. I whimper with protest when he pulls his finger all the way out, leaving me empty, but that objection turns to a moan when he proceeds to tie me to the bed posts, my arms and legs spread wide open, leaving me on full display. A giddy laugh bubbles up inside me.

"Look at you." He kneels on the bed and crawls between my legs, and I pull on the bindings, but in no way want to be free. No, I love being at his mercy and totally trust him with my body. "The perfect catch of the day," he says.

He lightly pets my sex, and his cock jumps, pre-cum pooling from the tip. I whimper, hating that it's going to drip onto my thigh instead of my tongue. So aware and connected with my needs and thoughts, he takes his cock into his hand.

"What, you want this?" he asks.

Instead of answering, I stick my tongue out.

"Fuck, yeah, you are so sexy." He straddles my body and shimmies upward, his cock only inches from my mouth.

"You know, I loved this sweet mouth wrapped around my cock in the limo, but this is so much better, babe. This way I get to see your expression and the pleasure on your face as you taste me." He taps my lips with the wet tip of his arousal. "You like sucking me, babe?"

"Yeah, I do," I say.

He brushes my hair back, and teases my tongue with his swollen crown. "That makes it all that much better." I lift my head, and suck on his cock, drinking all the come from his slit. "Jesus, you are so good at that."

"I never liked this before, Alek. Not until you," I admit.

His eyes soften as they meet mine, and warmth spreads over my skin as he tucks a strand of hair behind my ear. Honest to God, this man is the epitome of strength and power, yet he touches me with such tender need, such warmth and possession, it produces a fullness in my heart.

Desire twists inside me and I coil his ties around my wrists as he slides back down my body, his hair tickling my flesh, until my skin grows tight. His growl curls around me as he hungrily buries his mouth between my legs. He delves deep, sweeping his tongue over my clit and swollen flesh until a tremor shakes me to my core. The pleasure is so exquisite, my breath comes in ragged bursts, and I start coming again, all over his mouth.

My body clenches, and I quake from head to toe as I pulse and throb, this man touching me in places so deep, I fear I'll never be able to come back.

"Alek," I say, my voice a strangled whisper as he kisses a path up my stomach, until his mouth finds mine. I kiss him, and taste myself on his tongue.

"Yeah, babe?"

I can't seem to stop trembling, as he runs his rock hard cock along my slit.

"Inside me...please."

His hands press into the mattress on either side of my head, and his hips move, only to come to an abrupt halt. I whimper. "Please," I beg. "Please fuck me."

"Condom, hang on."

"No," I say, sheer desperation messing with my ability to think straight. "Just you, no barriers. I'm clean and I'm on the pill."

He smooths my hair back. "I'm clean, too. I promise."

"I know. I trust you."

He clenches down on his jaw, and with his body over mine, I can feel his heart slam in his chest. "Are you sure about this?" he asks, his voice low and harsh.

"It's what I want," I say, my stupid voice rough with emotion, and I pray to God it doesn't give too much away.

He reaches between my legs and inserts a finger. "You want me to fill your sweet pussy with my cum?"

I gulp, loving when he talks to me like this. "Yes," I murmur. "Or you could flip me over, and fill me somewhere else."

He lets out a shaky breath. "Aly," he says, his eyes moving over my face, like a soft, intimate caress. "You want my cock in your ass?"

"I want your cock everywhere, Alek," I say. Never in my life have I felt so cherished, so worshiped, and I want to give this man all of me.

For a long time, silence meets my words, then he shakes his head, and runs the back of his knuckles over my cheek. "You're...something else, babe," he whispers as his mouth finds mine. He kisses me deeply, and in one quick thrust, slides his cock into my sex. My hips lift, and while I want to touch him, being tied up and his to do with what he wants comes with its own pleasure.

My eyes slip shut as he fucks me, his beautiful cock gliding in and out until a shiver wracks my body and I'm miraculously coming again. My God, this man knows how to touch me. He stays inside me as I clench around him, and I open my eyes in time to see the pleasure on his face as he takes me over the edge again.

He reaches up and unties my hands, gently rubbing my wrists where the ties were binding me. A second later, my legs are free, and his voice is like an intimate caress when he says, "Roll over."

I do as he asks, and he puts a pillow under my hips. His growl curls around me as he grabs a fistful of my ass and squeezes. He falls over me and I enjoy the weight of him pressing down on me. He lightly runs his fingers over my arms, his breath hot on my back as he peppers me with kisses.

"If I had it my way, I'd never let you out of this bed," he murmurs, and shifts to the side, his raging hard cock, like steel against my leg. He reaches into his nightstand, and I turn to see the lube.

My throat tightens, but he touches me so softly, so gently, it reminds me that he'd never hurt me, and eases the nerves firing inside me

"You are so beautiful, Aly," he says and pours a generous amount of the cold lubrication between my cheeks. I gasp, but when he touches me, running his finger over my crevice. It warms me up and I settle against the pillow. "After today, I'll have been inside you everywhere," he says, and my eyes flick open at the hitch in his voice. I glance over my shoulder, and the desire reflecting in his eyes seeps under my skin and wraps around my heart. His smile is soft, and sure, and I smile back, completely ready for him.

He inches a finger into me. "Relax for me," he whispers, and kisses my back. He spends a long time widening me, stretching me and preparing me for his girth, as he works his finger into me, and presses me into the pillow to stimulate my clit.

His breathing is harsh as his warmth flows into my body, and soon enough I'm moving beneath him, writhing and anxious for his touch.

"Alek, please," I murmur, and he takes a sharp breath as he lifts my hips, and goes to his knees behind me.

I gasp as his fullness stretches me and he curses and stops. "Am I hurting you?" he asks, his voice low and soothing.

"No," I fib, wanting him to take me this way, wanting him to leave his mark on every inch of my body. He goes deeper and my fingers curl into the sheets, but I love this, I love every second of him owning my body like this. His hand is warm and soft on my back as he touches me, a quick check-in that I'm okay. Letting him know just how okay I am, I move my hips and he slides in deeper, filling me in a way I've never been filled.

"Jesus, Aly," he says and swallows, hard. "You are so tight."

He moves his hips, inching his cock out, and sliding in again. The sensations are different, a little overwhelming, actually, and I give myself over to them. He falls over me, moans against my shoulder. Shivers of warm need race through me, and the need in his touch, the way he's taking me, fills my heart with love.

He slips a hand between my hips and the pillow and applies pressure to my clit. I grind against his hand, and lift my ass to take him with each forward thrust. I have never felt so full. My pulse pounds against my neck, and fire licks a path up my thighs until the pleasure becomes so intense I let go again, unable to believe how many orgasms this man has wrung from my body.

"Oh, fuck yeah," he says his voice rough with desire as I clench around his cock. "I'm right there, babe."

"Fill me, Alek. I want all your cum inside me."

His hands find my hips and his fingers bite into my skin as he holds on to me like I'm the center of his universe. Happy tears sting my eyes as he calls out my name and lets go deep inside me, finding the pleasure he'd been chasing. I quiver at his hot release of pressure, revel in the sensations as he pulses inside my ass, filling me with every last drop.

Disoriented after that powerful climax, I gasp and close my eyes, waiting for the world to right itself around me. His body presses against mine, and we stay in that position for a long time. After a while, he pulls out, drags a blanket up to cover me.

"Stay put," he says, and if I had the energy to laugh, I would. I'm too weak, to sated to move. When he said he'd keep me here forever if he could, it could very well happen. I'm not sure I'll be able to move for a week.

He comes back and puts a warm cloth between my legs, and tears once again fill my eyes. The gesture is sweet and thoughtful and tugs at my emotions.

"Feel okay?" he asks.

"Never better," I manage to get out. He disappears again, and the next thing I know he's snuggling in beside me. He pulls me to him and arranges my body until I'm flush against his side, my head on his chest. My mind drifts, taking pleasure in the way he touched me with passion, and ownership, a delicate tenderness in his fingers that went well beyond the physical.

Everything inside me squeezes tight at the gentle display of affection. I lift my head to see him, and his drowsy expression is filled with pure adoration when it meets mine. Could he be any sweeter?

"Hey," he murmurs.

"Hey yourself," I say, trying for casual when my whole world is completely off balance.

He absently runs his fingers up and down my arm, leaving goosebumps.

"Do you want to have a nap while I get dinner ready?"

I yawn, completely drowsy, but I don't want to sleep. I want to spend all my time with this man. "No, I want to help."

"Tell you what. I'll pour you a glass of wine by the pool. You can relax while I barbecue dinner."

"You don't want my help?

"You caught the fish for us, babe. I'll do my part by cooking it for you."

Us.

My God, I love the sound of that. He touches my chin, lifts it. He leans down, pressing his mouth possessively on top of mine. My heart misses a beat as I give consideration to our future. Everything in the way he touches me and worships me speaks of something deeper. Is it possible that he might want the same thing I do? That after I finish Tyler's yard, we don't go our separate ways? What if I ask and I'm wrong?

What if I ask and I'm right?

Warm contentment fills my soul as Alyssa sips her wine in the pool and tosses the ball for Jack. He dashes off and his tail wags madly as he retrieves the ball and races back to the edge of the pool.

I grin as they play. "I thought he was a Jack Russell Terrier, not a retriever."

"He just has so much energy to burn off." She takes the ball from his mouth. "You like that, boy, you like that, huh?" she asks, and gives his head a quick rub before tossing the ball again.

He barks as he rushes off and she takes a sip of wine, sets it down and pushes off the side of the pool, completely naked beneath my watchful eye and completely comfortable in her own skin. I exhale slowly, happiness shimmering through me as I take in the view, thinking this is something I could totally get used to. Yeah, I'm a bachelor, a known player, and the guys have been telling me once the right girl comes along that will change it all. I never saw anything like that coming.

Until now.

Oh, boy.

"How's the trout?" she asks.

I arch one brow. "You say that like you're worried I'm going to burn it."

"Nope, just wondering."

"Liar," I shoot back, and she laughs before dunking under. I flip the fish on the grill, getting a good char on the sides. The delicious smells fill the backyard and my stomach takes that moment to growl. When she reemerges, I ask, "Should we save some for Gram?"

Her warm smile wraps around me. Christ, when she looks at me like that, all sweet and appreciative it fucks me over and makes me want to do things for her. "That's so sweet of you to think of her. She would love that."

"It's a big trout, plenty to go around. Of course, when I tell the story, it's going to be this big," I say and hold my hand about three feet apart, "and naturally it will be me who caught him and not you."

"If that's what your ego needs," she says, and I laugh with her.

"Nah, I'm just kidding. You've got mad fishing skills, babe. I'm impressed." Jack comes back with his ball, and I check the underside of the fish. "This is ready."

She glides to the stairs and water drips off her gorgeous bare body as she reaches for a towel and pats her skin. Once dry, she tugs on one of my T-shirts, which seem to be her favorite things to wear around the house. My favorite, too. My dick agrees. He's always clamoring for a front row seat.

I remove the fish, and we enter through the kitchen. Jack sniffs around and follows us in. Alyssa grabs the salad she made before jumping into the water and sets it on the table. We're both warm and relaxed, our moods mellow...sleepy.

She divvies up the salad and I portion out the trout, and we both lazily sit at the table. "Oh," she says, "I've finished with the sketches." She pushes her notepad toward me, and I look at the design ideas she has for the yard. "I wanted to add this fire pit and terrace, and this really nice rose garden with a fountain over here." She pauses and glances at me "I want to make this space his oasis, but I guess I probably should have discussed budget with him first."

I wave my fork, dismissively. "No budget, have at it."

"You can't be serious?"

"Why not?" I slide a generous portion of fish into my mouth and moan around it. "This is so good, Aly." She sits there and stares at me unblinkingly. "Aren't you going to eat?"

"You just told me I had an unlimited budget. That's insane." She stabs a cucumber and bites into it. "Who gives full control without approving a budget or design?"

"Insane people, obviously," I tease, and nudge her hand. "Now eat. You're going to need your energy for later."

She slides a piece of trout onto her fork. "I'll do whatever it takes to get him the best prices, but what I have in mind is not going to be cheap."

I shrug. "Whatever you do, Tyler will love it."

"You sure you don't want to call him and run this by him?"

"Nope, he trusts me, and I trust you, so there you go."

Excitement moves into her eyes. "I can really do all the things I want?" She bites into her trout and her eyes close over. "You cooked it perfectly."

"And you were worried about my skills," I say.

"You're a man of many talents, Alek."

"Don't you forget it."

She draws her bottom lip between her teeth, and her eyes have a dazed, distant look in them when she says, "Pretty sure there's no chance of that happening."

I jump up and refill her wine and snatch a cold beer for myself. She takes a sip, and the conversation turns to my friends who are coming for a visit this weekend.

"You must be looking forward to seeing them," she says. "I'll make myself scarce while they're here."

As soon as the words leave her mouth my stomach plummets. Shit, I don't want her to hide away, yet if I introduce her to my friends, how do I tell them to keep what a do a secret because I've been lying to her.

"No," I say. "I'd like you to meet them."

What are you doing, dude?

Fuck me.

She tucks a long strand of hair behind her ear, a seriousness in her eyes. "I don't want them to get the wrong idea, Alek."

"I'm a grown up. I can do what I want with who I want. It's not really their business."

She nods thoughtfully. "I guess you're right, and they must all clearly know this isn't serious. When we first met, you said your parents wanted you to settle down and have a family and you weren't interested in that. I'm sure they all know that about you, so maybe they won't jump to conclusions." She smiles sweetly. "You said they're always trying to set you up and get you married, so I just don't want them interrogating you, thinking there was more here."

"Right," I say. On one hand, it's sweet that she's worried about me, on the other, I'm fucking sick and tired of the reminder that we're not in a relationship.

What if I did want one, though?

You have a hockey career to think of, dude.

What if she came with me?

She's not going to leave her grandmother, and you'd never ask that of her.

As I mull that over, thinking there might be a solution in there, I remember that she doesn't really know who I am. Yeah, if that truth comes out now, I have no doubt she'd hate me for keeping it a secret.

I'm definitely going to have to talk to my friends, and Jesus, I'd better be prepared for the wrath of Quinn. She's a feisty little one, and she might think this situation calls for a good swift kick to my balls. She wouldn't be wrong.

"Okay," Alyssa says. "I'll stay and meet them." She grins. "I bet they're going to love to tell me salacious stories about you."

That's exactly what I'm worried about.

I check the time and redirect the conversation. "We'd better hurry if we want to try to catch Grandma awake."

"She's been doing so much better this last week. So alert." Her shoulders squeeze tight with happiness. "I love that you're getting to see that side of her."

"Me too," I say, understanding just how important her grandmother is to her.

"Afterward, I have a surprise for you," she says playfully.

"Does it involve you naked by any chance?"

She laughs. "No, but it might involve something long and hard."

"You had me at surprise, Aly."

We both finish our meals, rinse our plates and load the dishwasher. The place is tidy, as the cleaner was in this morning while Alyssa ran out to pick up some fresh flowers for her grandmother's vase. I offered to go with her but she insisted she had some business things to take care of, and I'm guessing it had to do with payments to the nursing home, so I let her have her privacy, even though being away from her was fucking torture.

Twenty minutes later, we walk into Rose's room, and she's sitting up, chatting with a woman with stylish silver hair and a big smile. The woman stands when she sees us.

"Alyssa, honey, there you are. I haven't seen you in a couple of weeks. You've been coming in a bit later than usual."

"I, uh, summertime," she says. "Always a busy time for me."

"Uh huh," the woman says as her gaze slides to me, and I fix my ballcap. "Who might this be."

"This is my friend Alek."

"Alek," Rose says, like she's still trying to place me.

"Alek, this is my grandma's friend Vivian. They've been friends since they were five years old."

I take her hand into mine and give it a small squeeze. "So nice to meet you, Vivian."

She grins at me, obviously very astute.

"What do you do, my boy?" she asks.

"Vivian," Alyssa says quickly. "He's helping a friend out in town. Dog watching for him."

She goes quiet for a long time, and I brace myself for an interrogation. "Well, any boy who likes dogs and is a friend of Alyssa's is a friend of mine." I relax a bit. "I should be on my way," she says. "Rose and I were working on a crossword puzzle." She turns to Rose, who sets the book on her nightstand. "We'll finish up when I come back tomorrow."

"You have fun with those grandkids, Viv," Rose says.

Vivian turns back to us. "Our grandkids from Boston are coming for a visit tonight."

"Oh, Alek is from Boston," Alyssa says.

Vivian nods, and her blue eyes narrow in on me. "Maybe that's why you look so familiar. Which part of Boston are you from?"

"West Roxbury."

"Oh, nice area." Her gaze scans my face, and I hope to fuck she doesn't place me. "My son is living in Dorchester. I must go. See you tomorrow night, Rose." As she gives her friends a hug, Alyssa removes the old flowers in the vase and adds new ones.

"So pretty," Rose says. "Now come sit, and tell me all about your day."

"I brought you fresh trout. I caught it and Alek cooked it."

"Oh, lovely."

Alyssa hands the container and fork over, and sits. I gesture that I'll grab us a couple cups of coffee. I step into the hall and make my way through the long corridor. There's an elderly gentleman at the coffee machine ahead of me, so I hang back. He seems to be having trouble trying to figure the machine out and when he glances over his shoulder, a measure of panic on his face, I step up to him.

"What are you looking for?" I ask.

"Coffee with cream," he says, and I press the buttons. The coffee pours, and I can feel his gaze drilling into me. "Aren't you—"

"Here you go," I say, keeping my head low and my hat over my eyes. "Careful, it's hot."

One hand with numerous dark spots takes the paper cup from me and I dig into my pocket, unease curling around me, filling me with the sense my world is about to come crashing down on me. Fuck man, here I thought Alyssa and I would just have some fun and I'd leave here without her ever needing to know who I was, but now... now everything is different.

With a cup of coffee in each hand I head back to the room when the man calls out, "Alek?"

I freeze for one brief second, but it's enough to give myself away. "Shit." I always stop to talk to my fans and give autographs, and I should this time, too. But I can't let Alyssa find out who I really am from someone else. I bite the inside of my cheek and continue on. I've seriously been enjoying the anonymity of this place, but I think it's soon going to come to an end.

I step back into the room, and Alyssa's head lifts from the book she'd been reading. She takes one look at me and her smile falls. Shit.

"Everything okay?"

"Yeah, fine," I say, and force a smile. "The machine was giving a guy a hard time. I had to help him." She nods, but doesn't look convinced as I hand her coffee over. She graciously accepts it and takes a big drink.

I kick back in my chair and pull my phone out to answer some emails and check in with the guys, who are asking if I'm coming to the cottage this summer. Alyssa would have a blast there, I'm sure of it. Swimming, hanging out, bonfires, and the girls all love to shop, and catch up. I'm certain they'd take her under their wing, but then I remember she's not going anywhere in a hurry, and that scenario is never likely to happen.

"All set?" Alyssa asks quietly and I lift my head to find her grandmother sleeping. Alyssa stretches out her arms and I stand, pulling her to me.

"You're tired," I say, and press my forehead to hers, enjoying the easy comfort between us.

"A bit, but I still have a surprise for you."

I brush my lips over hers, and when I catch movement from the corner of my eye I turn, and I swear to God, Rose just blinked her eyes shut. I stare at her for a moment. Is that a smirk on her face?

"Hey," Alyssa says, her hand on my cheek, and pulling my focus back to her. "Are you okay? You've been acting a little strange."

"I think Rose..." Alyssa's eyes narrow. "Nothing. I just... nothing." I take her hand. "Come on. Let's leave her to rest."

Alyssa scoops up her purse and we quietly leave the room. Back in her truck, she says, "Can we stop at my place for a second?" Her lips quick with excitement and I can't help but wonder what she's up to.

My cock twitches as understanding dawns. "Fuck, you're getting your girl scout outfit, aren't you?"

She whacks me. "No, but now that you mention it..." I step on the gas, go a little faster. "Easy there, Alek. Moxie needs a gentle touch."

When we finally pull into her driveway, I anxiously reach for the door handle. She puts her hand on my arm to stop me.

"Wait here, okay? I'll just be a second."

I nod, and turn the tunes up as she disappears inside her apartment. I glance around the area, and my mind goes to her grandmother's house. I can see why she wants to sell it, but damn, the look on her face when that couple had been checking it out damn near made me sob. Alyssa comes from the building with two hockey sticks in her hand, and I swear to fucking God, my heart just grew twice the size as it climbs into my throat.

Could this woman be any sweeter? I jump from the truck, and she's grinning from ear-to-ear as I meet her at the hood. "This is what you were up to this morning when you didn't want me to come with you?" I ask.

"Yup. I taught you to fish, now you're going to teach me how to play hockey."

"You bought these...to surprise me." No way can I let her pay for them.

"Technically, I didn't buy them. I borrowed them from Mr. Landry, an old family friend. He has tons of kids and grandkids." She laughs and says, "He's always trying to set me up with his grandson who lives in New York."

A spark of jealousy rages through me, so sharp and fierce it catches me by surprise. I suck air in through my nose, and my hands fist at my sides. Honest to God the thoughts of this woman with any other man but me, is an image I don't want floating around inside my brain.

So, what are you going to do about it, Alek?

"Are you okay?" she asks, and puts her hand on my shoulder, as her worried gaze moves over my face. She touches my forehead. "You're not getting sick, are you? You seem a bit pale, and earlier at the nursing home—"

"I'm fine, Aly," I push past the massive lump in my throat "Just…this was so sweet."

She rolls her eyes to make light of it. "They're just hockey sticks, Alek. I didn't part the sea for you," she says, and I drag her to me. Giving all of zero fucks that an elderly couple just climbed from their vehicle and are now watching us, I hold the back of her head and bring her lips to mine for a soft kiss. Fuck, I love the way she sags against me, her body meshing with mine so perfectly. Her eyes are soft and half-lidded when I break the kiss and take the sticks from her.

I toss them into the back, and open the passenger side door for her. She slides in and fixes her mussed hair as I circle the front and jump in.

"You want to learn how to play hockey, huh?"

"I think it will be fun?"

"I'm a goalie," I tell her.

"Oh, that's your favorite position?"

"I have lots of favorite positions, Aly, but on the ice, I'm a goalie."

She thinks about that for a second. "How about this? We play, and if I score on you, I win. If I can't score on you, you win."

"Interesting. But you know I always play to win, right? And there is no way you're going to score on me, babe."

She rolls her shoulders, like she's not worried. "There's a first for everything."

"Okay, so what's my prize?"

She reaches across the seat, takes my hand and puts it on her thigh. Her arousal reaches out to me. "Whatever position *you* want, later tonight."

My cock jumps, ready to take that bet. "What do you win?"

"Whatever position *I* want. And let me tell you, I have something pretty twisty in mind."

"Fuck," I say, and shake my head, feigning distress.

Eyes wide her body stiffens. "What?"

"It's in my nature to play to win, but now I don't know what to do," I give her a playful wink. "Not when you put a twist on it like that."

ALYSSA

I'm crouched down in the backyard elbow-deep into planting a shrub when a small laugh escapes my lips. Last night, playing hockey with Alek was a blast. He let me get a few shots in the net—on purpose. He denies it, but I had him at twisty. Later that night he took me hard and deep as I bent over the bed, and offered myself up to him.

The sound of a car door slamming reaches my ears, and pulls my thoughts back. My stomach lurches, and I steal a fast glance over my shoulder, but can't see the driveway from my position. Honestly, I have no idea why the thoughts of meeting Alek's friends has me so anxious. It's not like I want or need them to like me because I'm in a lifelong relationship with Alek. I'm not, and I'll likely never set eyes on them again after this weekend.

Is that what you want, Alyssa?

No, it's not what I want, not even close. He said he's between jobs, but maybe he can get one here. Maybe he can stay. My heart races at that thought. Do I dare hope that it's something he might consider?

I push to my feet, take a fueling breath and brush my hair

from my face, wanting to look a bit presentable. I head toward the front of the house and circle Alek's old car, which has been sitting in the driveway beside Moxie for weeks now. We've been taking my truck everywhere. I think Alek likes driving her.

My steps slow when I see Alek in deep conversation with his friends, his muscles so tense, I'm worried something is going to snap. I have no idea what he's saying. I can't hear him from my distance, but whatever it is, it seems pretty serious. My stomach tightens even more, and I'm about to back track, disappear into the backyard to give them space when the woman, who I assume is Quinn, lifts her head, her blue eyes locking on mine. A wide smile splits her lips and she pushes past Alek.

"You must be Alyssa," she says, her warm and welcoming arms wrapping around me.

"And you must be Quinn. I've heard a lot about you."

She turns and glares at Alek. "And here we've not heard anything about you," she says, a scolding tone in her voice.

"There's nothing really to tell," I say. "Alek and I are just friends."

She winks at me. "Yeah, Jonah and I were just friends once too." She snorts out a laugh. "Actually, we were frenemies."

"Really?"

"Yeah, I had to help him out with my niece who we thought was his child." She waves her hand. "Never mind, it's all very complicated, and we're here to relax and have some downtime."

"Mommy, mommy, I want to play with Captain Jack," her son Scotty yells from his dad's arms.

Quinn puts her arm around mine. "Come on, I'll introduce you to my boys."

"I'm going to get you all dirty," I say, noting her clean

shorts and pretty blouse. I'm in muddy coveralls. Damn, maybe I should have changed and been a little more presentable when meeting them, but Quinn doesn't make me feel uncomfortable at all in my work wear.

She shrugs, and blows it off. "I have a husband and a son. I'm used to dirt."

Laughing, I fall into step with her, instantly liking her. She leads me to Alek and Jonah, and I note the frown on Jonah's face, but it disappears when he turns his attention from Alek to me.

"Hey Alyssa, nice to meet you. Alek says you're redoing Tyler's yard." He glances around. "About time he did something with the place."

"And this little guy is Scotty," Quinn says as Jonah sets him down. "Scotty, Alyssa is Alek's friend."

"Hi," he says, and hops back and forth, clearly anxious to play with the dog.

"Nice to meet you, Scotty," I say.

"You have dirt on your face," he says and points.

I chuckle. "That's because I was playing in the dirt."

"I want to play in the dirt too," he says, and laughs.

"I think Captain Jack is inside waiting to play with you. You know, he has a favorite ball, and if you throw it, he'll run and get it and bring it back to you."

His eyes go big, and my heart thumps. His enthusiasm hits my stupid maternal clock, and the sudden thoughts of never fulfilling bucket list number six, raising a family of my own in Grandma's big old house, hits like a punch.

Alek puts his hand on my back, like he can feel the war waging inside me. I lean into him, absorbing his familiar warmth and comfort.

"You're good with kids," Quinn says. "You'll be a great mom someday."

I nod, and bite the inside of my cheek, an effort to hide the storm roiling through me.

Alek's hand tightens on my back, and I smile up at him. His dark eyes move over my face. "Do you have more work to do, or do you want to come in and hang out with us? I was just going to get the barbecue going," Alek says.

"I need about thirty minutes," I say, wanting to give him some time with his friends alone.

"Alyssa, do you need any help?" Quinn asks.

"No, I'm good, but thanks." I smile at Quinn. Not only is she beautiful, with the prettiest blue eyes I've ever seen, she's sweet and thoughtful. My stomach squeezes. I'd really like to have a friend like her in my life.

She takes her son's hands. "I'll take Scotty inside to play with Captain Jack, and you boys can get caught up," Quinn says.

I step back, giving the guys privacy and can feel Alek's gaze on my back as I round the corner. I take a quick breath when I'm alone. Why the hell am I suddenly so emotional? Oh, maybe because the man I'm falling for is leaving soon, and I have to sell my grandmother's place, and little Scotty reminded me of all the things I want and will likely never have. Why the hell did I ever get involved with Alek? I should have known better. I am so goddamn stupid, but the truth is, before Alek, I wasn't really living. I was surviving, going through the motions of the day to day. I don't want to do that anymore. I want to make a life here with Alek, I want him to stay. I pick up the shovel and drive it into the ground.

"Hey, you okay?" Alek asks.

I jump and spin around. "You frightened me. I didn't hear you coming."

He touches my face. "Sorry." He leans in and lightly brushes his lips over mine. "Everything okay, Aly?"

"Yeah sure," I say injecting a lightness into my voice, but

the frown on his forehead lets me know he doesn't believe me. "Your friends are great."

"They like you too."

I nod, happy to hear that.

He jerks his thumb over his shoulder. "You seemed a little upset about something back there."

I briefly close my eyes. "Oh great. I made an idiot of myself in front of your friends."

"No, you didn't," he says. "I'm the only one that noticed. Are you sure you're okay?"

"Meeting new people. I'm not always great at it," I say.

He grins. "Yeah, you hated me when we met."

"I didn't hate you. You rear-ended me when I was in a hurry and then you went all alpha on me."

His arm slides around my back and he pulls me against him. "I thought you liked it when I went alpha?"

Heat moves through me. "Oh, I do."

"And I thought we were going to stop saying rear-ended," he says, his hand sliding down to grab my ass. He gives a squeeze and I yelp.

"Stop, before your friends see."

"They're getting settled in their room."

"Are you guys okay?" I ask. "You all seemed to be in a pretty deep conversation when they first arrived."

He takes a fast breath and scrubs his face as he lets it out. "Yeah, we just had some things we needed to talk about." He looks past my shoulder, his eyes narrowed and I can almost hear the wheels spinning. "Aly, we need—"

He stops and turns at the sound of Scotty shrieking and Captain Jack barking and chasing the ball.

"You wanted to say something?" I ask.

"We need to talk, but it can wait until later," he says.

My heart lurches. Do I dare hope he wants to talk about a future?

"You want some help here?" he asks.

"No, go," I say and back up an inch when the dog runs circles around us and Quinn chases after Scotty. "Hang out with your friends. I'll be in shortly."

I watch him walk off, and go back to finishing what I'm doing. Once I get the shrub planted, I head inside to shower. By the time I finish, I hear laugher out by the pool so I head outside to join Alek and his friends. Quinn's smile is wide and inviting as she pushes a chair out for me and holds up a bottle of wine.

"Tell me you're joining me," she says.

"I'm joining you." I laugh when she pours a generous amount and slides it my way. She takes a sip of hers and exhales.

"I have to say, it's so nice to have a girl to talk to. Usually I'm stuck listening to all the guy talk and guy barks," she says with a laugh when Scotty and Captain Jack dart by. "So you're a landscape artist," she says. "That's so interesting."

"I really enjoy it," I say and take a sip of the wine. "I'm excited to be doing Tyler's yard. I have so many ideas. I hear you own a daycare?"

"It's true, I'm insane, but please don't hold that against me."

I laugh. "I think it's great."

She stares at me. "I wouldn't go so far as to say that, but if you're ever in Boston, come by, I'll show you around, take you to lunch."

"Maybe I will," I say, but I know that's not ever going to happen.

Alek and Jonah are chatting by the grill, and Alek tosses the steaks on. My stomach takes that moment to grumble.

"They're good friends huh?" I ask.

"Yeah, they go way back," she says.

"What does Jonah do?" I ask.

Her gaze darts to Alek, her eyes drilling into him, and he stares back, shifting like he's uncomfortable about something. Quinn's lips thin, when she says, "He's sort of in between things right now."

I stiffen. Okay, clearly it's not something she wants to talk about. I steal a fast glance at Alek, and his brow is tight, like he's tormented by something as he shifts his focus back to the grill and Quinn leans into me all conspiratorial like, making me feel like I belong here with them all.

"So you and Alek, huh?"

"We're friends."

"Friends with benefits," she states and grins. "It's okay. I'm not judging. I think it's great."

"You do?"

"Sure." She runs her fingers over the stem of her glass and says, "But I have to tell you something. I've never seen him look at a woman the way he looks at you."

"You've seen him with many women?" I ask, and hate the wave of jealousy gripping my gut.

She shrugs. "Yeah, but he's never been serious." She taps her chin. "He's never introduced us to anyone before, and having someone live with him." She shakes her head, her blue eyes wide. "Unheard of." She leans back in her chair. "But I can definitely see what he likes in you."

I coil a strand of hair around my finger. "Thanks."

"You like him too, right?"

I angle my head, take in the amazing man standing in front of the grill. My heart wobbles, and even if I was an Oscar-winning actress, I'm not sure I could hide my feelings from Quinn. "Yeah, I like him," I say. "He's a really nice guy."

"His heart is in a good place, but sometimes he doesn't always make the best decisions. I want you to remember that," she says her face deadly serious.

"Ah, okay," I say, even though I have no idea what she's talking about.

"How do you like your steak, Quinn?" Alek asks, like he's trying to break up our conversation, which is strange. Doesn't he want us to bond? Or maybe he's worried she's going to spill all his secrets.

"You know how I like my steak, Alek," she says and snarls at him again. Jeez, does she even like him?

"Alyssa, would you mind grabbing the salads from the fridge?" Alek asks.

I stand. "Sure."

"I'll help," Quinn says, and gives Alek a bump as she walks past. I can't help but think she's pissed off at him for something, but I don't ask because it's none of my business.

"Alek mentioned you have a grandmother here in town," Quinn says as I pull open the fridge.

"I do." I gesture to the utensil drawer. "Would you mind grabbing knives and forks?"

She pulls open the drawer. "It's nice that you visit her every night."

"She means a lot to me."

She puts her hand on my arm. "I'm sorry you have to sell her house."

I shake my head, surprised. "How much did Alek tell you?"

"Oh, he told me a lot," she says, like she's pissed again.

We head back outside and set the table. I put the salads in the middle. The doorbell rings.

"Who could that be?" I ask, and step inside to answer. I make my way to the door, and open it.

"About time—" the guy stops talking, his head jerking back as his gaze slides over me. "Oh, hey, sorry. I figured Alek would be answering."

"You're a friend of Alek's?" I ask as I take in his longish

dark hair, and his nice blue eyes. My God, Alek has some seriously good looking friends, but to me, no one could ever compare to him.

"Yeah, I was visiting a buddy in Boston, and heard Jonah and Quinn were here. Thought I'd surprise them all."

"Come in."

"Ah, am I interrupting something?"

"Nope, everyone is out back. Let's go surprise them."

He follows me down the hall. "I'm Alyssa, by the way."

"Cason," he says. "Cason Callaghan."

"How do you know these guys?" I ask and glance at him over my shoulder.

He gives me a strange look, and scratches his face. "Hockey," he says, and Alek and Jonah smile in surprise when we step outside.

"What the hell are you doing here?" Alek asks, and pulls him in for a hug.

"Can't be a party without me," Cason says and holds his hands out. I smile at him. He's super cute, big and athletic like Alek and Jonah.

He gives Jonah and hug, and I catch the worry in Alek's eyes as they flash to me. "I see you met Alyssa," Alek says.

"Sort of."

Alek cracks a beer and hands it to Cason. "She's a landscape artist, doing the lawn for Tyler."

"Oh yeah," Cason says as he smiles at me. "You're not one of Tyler's sisters?"

"No, I'm a local," I say.

"A landscaping artist, huh? That's a cool job," he says. "I'd love to hear more about it."

Cason pulls a chair out beside me and plunks down into it, and his warm scent of soap and fabric softener reach my nose. "Ever get out to Seattle? I could always use a great landscape artist. Just bought a place."

"You live in Seattle?" He nods, and I can't help but think he's far from home. "I always wanted to visit."

"Sure, and now that I have a new place, you've got yourself a place to stay."

"Back off, Cason," Quinn says, and rolls her eyes.

"What?" he says with a laugh.

"You're such a troublemaker."

"That's why they call me the troublemaker," he says, and my gaze goes back and forth between the two. Clearly, I'm missing an inside joke here.

Alek hands the tongs to Jonah, and a look I don't understand passes between them before Alek turns his attention to Cason.

"Cason, can I see you inside," Alek says.

Cason pushes from the chair, and the two step inside. "What's that all about?" I ask Quinn, who is glaring at Alek's back.

"I don't think Alek likes Cason hitting on his girl," she says.

His girl.

Damn I like the sound of that.

She puts her hand on mine and gives it a squeeze. Big blue eyes search my face in an almost comforting way. "I also think you two need to talk, Alyssa."

I look into her blue eyes, and my heart jumps into my throat as dread takes hold. I swallow uneasily and inch back in my seat, the feeling that something very bad is about to happen rushing through my blood like a runaway freight train ready to go off the track.

ALEK

I take my last bite of steak, and somehow manage to get it past the lump in my throat. Even though every part of my being is fucking terrified that I've messed this up with Alyssa, we need to talk sooner rather than later. I hated asking my friends to keep my secret—Quinn looks like she's ready to neuter me—but she needs to hear it from me, and I have to figure out how to tell her without her hating me.

From across the table, Scotty is telling some story about Daisy, Zander's daughter, and everyone laughs at his antics. Alyssa seems quite taken with the boy in much the same way my buddy Cason was taken with her. Fuck, I had to shut that shit down, fast. Cason is a great guy, one of the greatest I know, but he had to know Alyssa was off limits.

Is she though?

When it comes right down to it, I have no claim on her. We agreed to a summer fling, nothing more and by rights if she wants to go out with Cason she can. It will just have to be over my dead body.

"Who wants to hit up the pub?" Cason asks. "Shoot a couple games of pool?"

Jonah looks at Quinn and she waves her hand. "Go, Scotty and I are going to go for a swim and then I'll get him settled in for the night. Maybe we can all play cards or a board game when you get back. Alyssa, do you like cards?"

Alyssa smiles, like she's so happy to be included. My heart hurts for the beautiful woman, inside and out, who's never really been a part of a family, and damned if I don't want to offer mine up to her. She needs this, deserves this, and there is nothing I want more for her.

Jonah leans over and gives her a kiss. "Sounds like a plan."

Alyssa sets her napkin down. "I have to go visit my grandmother, but I'd love to play some games when I get back."

"I'll go with you," I say. "Maybe we'll have time to talk alone on the drive."

"Nope," she says quickly. "You go shoot pool with your friends."

I don't look at Quinn. I can feel her gaze drilling into me. "Are you sure?"

"Of course. I'll tell Grandma you said hello."

She picks up her plate and reaches for the others. "Leave them," Quinn says. "I can take care of these."

Alyssa gives her a grateful smile, and she disappears inside. All eyes turn to me, and I pinch the bridge of my nose.

"Yeah, I know," I say and jump up. I head inside, and Alyssa is grabbing her purse.

"Hey," I say and wrap my arms around her, pulling her back to my chest.

She rests her head against my chest, and I drop a kiss onto her head. I breathe in her warm scent and my heart pounds against my chest.

"We won't be long," I say to her, and she turns in my arms.

"I won't be either." She goes up on her toes and presses her lips to mine. "See you soon," she says, but then her head angles toward me. "Are you okay?"

"Yeah, I'm good," I say, and rake my hand through my hair. With my friends outside, and her on the way to see her grandmother, now is not the time to tell her who I really am. "We'll talk later, okay?"

"Yeah, okay," she says, and I give her another kiss before she heads out the door. I head back to the kitchen and find Quinn leaning against the counter, her arms folded.

"I know," I say to her.

"I like her, Alek."

"I like her too."

"Yeah, so you need to talk to her," she says.

"She's going to hate me. Jesus, Quinn, if she does a search on me, she's probably not going to like what she sees."

Quinn's face softens and she pushes off the counter. She places her hands on my shoulders. "You're a good guy, Alek, and what you did in your past is your past." Her gaze moves over my face. "Why did you keep it from her?"

"I liked the way she was around me."

She nods. "I get it. I really do. So, what are you going to do now? What do you want out of all this?"

"I never thought I'd fall for her," I say, and she smiles. "I thought we'd just have some fun, and go our separate ways, but I…I fell in love with her, Quinn."

She goes up on her toes, throws her arms around me and gives me a big hug. "Then that's what you need to tell her."

"You're right."

She goes back on her feet when the guys all come in. Jonah looks at me, his face contorted like he knew Quinn was going to tear me a new one.

"We can clean this up when we get back," I say to Quinn as Scotty tugs at her shirt, asking to go for a swim.

"You guys go, have fun."

We head out, climb into Cason's vehicle and head to town. The guys chat, but I'm too lost in my thoughts to add to the conversations. Fifteen minutes later, we're all sipping on beer, and shooting pool, all anonymity gone now that the three of us are together.

A couple of women come over and begin to flirt with us. Any other time, I would have been all over that, much like Cason is right now, but I've lost all appeal for one-night stands. There is only one girl I want to go to bed with at night, and more importantly wake up to the next morning.

Jonah holds his hand up to showcase his wedding ring when one of the girls sidles up to him. He shoots me a grin. "My buddy Alek is a free man," he says, fucking me over and I produce my middle finger. He laughs and takes a shot. Soon more people crowd around us and before we know it, we're giving autographs.

I finish signing, and getting my picture taken, when a guy I recognize from Greenleaf, I think his name was Eli, comes up to me. "You know I thought that was you when I saw you with Alyssa." He puts his hand on my back and laughs. "She never let the secret out," he adds, and worry worms its way through my veins. I talk to him for a few more minutes and step up to the guys.

"I have to go," I say. "I'm going to walk over to the nursing home."

Jonah pats me on the back. "Good luck, buddy."

I step out into the night, and take a fueling breath. No way can I let her leave the nursing home and risk her running into someone from the pub. She needs to hear it from me. I hurry my steps and breathe a sigh of relief when I spot her truck still in the parking lot. Inside, I sign in and make my way to her grandmother's room. I hear three voices and poke my head in to find Alyssa, Rose and Rose's friend, Vivian.

A smile lights up Alyssa's face when she sees me. "Alek, what are you doing here?"

"Oh, it's the charmer," Vivian says grinning. "Come on in. Don't just stand there."

"The charmer," Rose says, her eyes falling over me as I cross the room. I swallow uneasily as she narrows her eyes and scrutinizes me. "The charmer," she says again, and her mouth drops open. "The puck charmer," she says again, and my heart falls into my stomach.

"Oh my," Vivian says, and gives Alyssa a little whack. "Why didn't you tell us who he was."

Alyssa shakes her head. "I did tell you. It's Alek."

"That's not what I mean," Vivian says. "You didn't tell us he was the puck charmer. Always wearing that ball cap to hide his face."

"I have no idea what you're talking about."

"He's the goalie for the Seattle Shooters," Rose says.

"But of course, you already knew that," Vivian says with a laugh. "Now I'm going to need your autograph."

Alyssa's gaze slides to mine, and her eyes are confused. "What's going on?"

"Alyssa," I say softly. "Can we talk."

"Alek?" she says. "Are you a professional hockey player?"

"Alyssa, can we go out into the hall?"

She pulls her phone from her purse and her eyes grow wide as she runs her fingers over the screen. "You're Alek Matthews, goalie for the Seattle Shooters. I can't believe this."

"You didn't know?" Vivian asks.

Her face pales as her eyes dart to Rose and Vivian, who are watching the worst day of my life unfold.

"No," she says, her voice a bit shaky.

Vivian turns on me. "Why wouldn't you tell her?"

"If I could just talk to Alyssa alone for a minute."

"What does puck charmer mean? Why do they call you that?" Alyssa asks.

"You know what they call the girls who hang out with hockey players?" Vivian asks.

"Puck bunnies..." Her eyes cast down for a brief second. "You're the puck bunny charmer."

"It's just a name, Alyssa. Cason actually gave it to me."

"Cason, another player for the shooters and Jonah...Quinn said he was in between jobs." She jumps up and covers her face. "Oh my God, everyone knew but me. You had your friends lying," she says her voice bordering on hysteria. "Oh my God, I'm a joke."

I take a step toward her, but she holds her hands up to stop me. "Don't."

"She meant he was in between seasons."

"That's not what any of you meant. You were lying to me, and they all backed you up." A sound crawls out of her throat, a half laugh, a half groan. "I must be the laughingstock. I can't believe this. Why would you do this?"

"I liked you, Alyssa," I say.

She gives a humorless laugh. "You sure have a funny way of showing it." She looks around. "What was this, Alek? Slumming for the summer, hanging out with a local for a good time?"

"It's not like that, Alyssa. I didn't know I was going to fall for you."

"Fall for me. You fell for me. How can I believe anything that comes out of your mouth? Wait, so you're telling me that you never would have told me? That you would have just left here, leaving me none the wiser of who you really were?"

"I...well..." Jesus, how the fuck do I answer that, because early on, that really was my intention. I am such a fuck-up.

Guilt twists inside me as she stands there, staring at me, paralyzed by the truth.

My stomach plummets

"I messed up, Alyssa."

"Is this what you wanted to talk to me about? Tell me you were pretending to be someone else, and that you had a career to get back to when you were done slumming."

"I was never slumming. It wasn't like that."

"Oh, it was like that. Otherwise you would have been honest with me, Alek. You know honesty is important to me." She points to the door. "Leave. I never want to see you again."

"Can we talk? Let me explain this right, so you can understand."

"I understand perfectly and don't want to hear anything you have to say, now or ever. Go, go back to Seattle or wherever the hell it is you live, and tell Tyler he's going to need to hire someone else."

"But…the job, the money. You need—"

"Oh my God, am I some charity case to you? Is this some sort of payment for services rendered, Alek?"

"It's not like that at all." He clenched down on his jaw with an audible click. "If you'll give me a minute."

"I've wasted enough minutes with you," she says. "Leave." She shakes her head and adds, "You think I'd be used to people leaving, but I guess it never gets easier."

"I don't want to go."

"Come on, Alek," she shoots back. "You never had any intentions of staying, and I never should have thought you might."

"You wanted me to stay, then? There was a time you wanted me to stay?" he asks a measure of hope filling his eyes.

"Wanted, as in past tense."

I glance at Rose and Vivian, who are staring at me, their lips a thin line of white, their hands clasped together tightly.

I open my mouth, but Rose glares at me. "Leave," she says. "You're not welcome here."

I take a breath and swallow it. With my heart drowning in

the pit of my stomach, I turn around and walk away from the only girl I wanted to give the world to, and instead, gave her every reason in the world to hate me. Could I have fucked this up anymore?

With my head down, I walk outside, and instead of going back to the pub, I make my way home on foot, needing the air to help clear my head. By the time I make it back, Scotty is in bed, and Quinn is flicking through the stations.

"You guys are back early," she says.

"It's just me."

She turns her head, takes one look at my sorry ass, and flicks off the television.

"Oh, no," she says and climbs to her feet. "Alek...what happened?"

"It didn't go so well."

I plunk down onto the sofa and bury my face in my hands. "I totally fucked it up, Quinn. I love her and now I've lost her. I should have just told her right from the start."

She sits on the coffee table facing me, her blue eyes big and worried. "There has to be a way to fix this. Alyssa is a smart girl. She'll understand why you did what you did. I'm sure she's going to give you a second chance."

I shake my head, doubting that. My God, the hurt in her eyes, hurt I put there, feels like a fist to the gut. "I lied to her. She hates liars."

"But she loves you, Alek, and while you hurt her, deep inside she knows your heart is in the right place."

"Do you think so?"

"I know so. She might just need a little time."

"I love her, Quinn," I say, as tears pound behind my eyes. "I fucking love her and I've never loved any woman before."

"I saw you two together. I could see the love on her face, and on yours. You two belong together. Of that I have no doubt. You can't leave here, Alek, not without making this right between you two."

"Her whole life, people have walked out on her, left her behind, and let her down. I never wanted to be one of those people. I want to be the guy she can count on, the one that's going to stick around for the long haul." I grab a fistful of my hair. "But now…"

"Now you have to figure out how to make this right?"

"As much as she hates people leaving, she told me to leave and never come back."

She puts one hand on my knee and gives it a squeeze. "So what are you going to do about that?"

"I don't know. She won't even listen to me."

"Then you need to do something, something big that will give her no choice but to listen."

"How…what?"

"Maybe you need to show her you're not like those other people. Maybe you need to show her you're sorry, and no matter what, you're not going to leave, even if she's pushing you away."

My throat is so tight, it hurts, making it hard to talk. "How am I supposed to do that?"

"You're a smart guy, Alek," she says softly. "I bet you can figure it out."

18

ALYSSA

It's been two long days since I've set eyes on Alek, and even though I'm hurt and angry, I'm still mourning his absence. After I kicked him out of the nursing home, I went home and ate a tub of ice cream and wallowed in self-pity until I fell asleep crying. Ridiculous, I know, but I thought we had more, thought we had a closeness, an intimacy that went beyond a summer fling. Thought there was something blossoming between us, but the only thing blossoming were the flowers I planted in Mrs. Henderson's yard.

I should have known better. I let down my guard and let him in, and I want to say he's no better than anyone else in my life, but I can't say that. He never once led me to believe we were going to have more, or that he might want to stay. No, I made that all up in my head. But I still don't get why he kept his identity a secret. What was the point in that?

I walk through the nursing home and sign in. I lift my head, catching movement in the corner of my eye. My heart lurches when I glance at the exit door banging shut. Alek? I blink, sure I'm seeing things, and when I walk to the door to look out, he's not there. Damn, I must be hallucinating.

Flowers in hand, I head to Grandma's room and she's sitting up, a smile on her face as she talks to Vivian.

"Darling, how are you?" Vivian asks. Grandma holds her hand out to me.

I close the gap between us, take her frail hand in mine, and my heart pinches tight as I give her a comforting squeeze.

"I'm great," I lie, but I fear they can easily see through it. Heck, my eyes are still puffy and red from all the tears, and I look like I haven't combed my hair in days. "How are you both doing?"

"Oh, we're just fine," Vivian says.

Grandma looks at me. "Have you talked to Alek?"

"No," I say and turn from her to fix the flowers. Fresh tears threaten. I don't want her to see that I'm still shaken up. She worries enough about me as it is.

"That's a good thing," she says. "He was a horrible person."

"Well, he wasn't horrible, Grandma." I recall the first day he hit my car and insisted on helping. Even after I snuck out the next day, he'd showed up at Greenleaf, wanting to do all the heavy lifting because he was worried about me. "I mean, he helped me for weeks, and was really...sweet."

"Too much sweet can give you a toothache," Vivian says. "No one needs that in their life."

"The Puck Charmer," Grandma says. "He was probably stringing you along and hitting on all the women in town."

"Actually, he wasn't doing that," I say. When he was with me, which was all the time—he never wanted me out of his sight—I was his sole focus. My God, no man had ever looked at me the way he did, making me feel like I was the most important woman in the world. Could that be faked?

"He's no good," Vivian says. "Tricking you into falling for him." Vivian eyes me and lowers her voice to add, "Tricking you into his bed." She makes a tsking sound. "Men these days."

I cringe. I do not want to be talking about my sex life with these two, but I can't let them think what happened was all on him. "He never tricked me," I say, and think back. I was the one who wanted him, who decided to seduce him. He straight up told me he didn't want to sleep with me and ruin things between us because he liked being with me. God, I loved being with him.

"Wearing that hat all the time so no one recognized him," Grandma says with a shake of her head. "Here I thought that boy loved all the attention. Must have been hiding for other reasons."

My mind goes back to his friend Tyler. What was it Alek said that first day?

"I guess all the media attention got to him and he just wants to fly under the radar. That's understandable, don't you think?"

I agreed with him. Who wants to go around all the time with a camera shoved in their face, never able to have a normal conversation with anyone without someone bothering you, or wanting something from you?

"Maybe he just wanted to fly under the radar," I say.

Is that why he never told me? He just liked what we had between us, like me not knowing who he was.

"Doesn't matter." Vivian waves her finger in a scolding manner. "He should have told you."

"You're right," I say. "He should have told me." But there's a small part of me that's beginning to understand why he didn't. I drop down into the chair and feel two sets of eyes on me as I lean forward and press my palms to my eyes as my mind goes back to my conversation with Quinn.

"His heart is in a good place, but sometimes he doesn't always make the best decisions. I want you to remember that."

"No one deserves a second chance, Alyssa," Grandma says, and that's when I get what they're doing.

Sneaky old ladies!

I lift my head. "Was Alek just here?" Need gathers in a knot in my stomach simply from mentioning his name. They both look away and avoid my question. "Was he here?" I ask again.

"Might have been," Vivian says and points to her head. "My memory isn't what it used to be."

"Why was he here?" I demand, and jump from my seat. "What did he want?"

"Can't remember," Grandma says. "You might have to ask him that yourself."

"Maybe I will," I say when my cell phone rings. I grab my purse, my heart leaping. Could it be Alek? My stomach sinks when I see it's a call from the realtor. Maybe that young couple I spotted admiring the place decided to put in an offer. A mixed bag of emotions hit like a brick. On one hand, I'm relieved that I'm selling to help pay the bills, but on the other, there's sadness that the one place I felt loved and wanted is no longer going to be a part of my world. It guts me.

I slide my finger across the phone, and catch the strange way Grandma is eyeing me. What does she know that I don't? My realtor, Mr. Marshall lets me know we have an offer and I nod, fighting back the tears pounding behind my eyes. I hang up and try for my brightest smile.

"Good news, Grandma. We have an offer on the house. That was Mr. Marshall asking me to meet him to sign the papers."

Grandma claps her hands together in joy, and Vivian says, "I do love it when a plan comes together."

"I better go," I say and give Grandma a kiss before heading out the door. Even though it's only a short distance, I hop into Moxie and drive her to Grandma's old homestead. I swallow hard and struggle to keep myself together when I pull into the driveway. I don't see Mr. Marshall's vehicle, but it's possible he walked here.

I hop from Moxie and head up the driveway. The door is unlocked, so I enter and call out, "Hello?" At first my voice is met with silence, but when I hear footsteps, I shut the door behind me and head down the hall and toward the kitchen. Warm memories flood me as I breathe in the familiar scents in the house, take in the furniture that's been left to give it a warm, cozy feeling for viewings.

"Hello, Mr. Marshall?" I call out in the kitchen, and spin around, coming face to face with none other than Alek Matthews, aka, The Puck Charmer. "What...what are you doing here?" I ask, the mere sight of him fraying the tattered edges of my heart just a little more. I take a few fast breaths, working to keep it together.

"Hi," he says softly, his gaze carefully moving over my face, like he's worried I'm going to bolt.

I pinch the bridge of my nose. "Alek, what is going on? Why were you at the nursing home?"

"Oh, you know about that?"

He comes a bit closer, and his warmth and familiarity curl around me. I hug myself, when what I really want is for him to pull me into his arms and tell me everything is going to be all right.

"So you *were* there." I shake my head as my brain rattles around inside my skull, trying to make sense of all this.

"Do you remember when I said I'd never purposely hurt you?"

"Yes," I say and reach out to grip the counter.

"I meant it, Aly. I'd never purposely do anything to hurt you. I'm sorry. So fucking sorry I never told you who I really was." He grabs a fistful of hair and tugs. "The thing is, I really like you. I liked the way you were with me when we first met. Natural. Yourself. You never tried to impress me, never wanted anything from me," he grins and adds, other than my body. I shouldn't smile. I don't want to smile, but my lips quirk at his cuteness, my heart spilling over with the love I have for him. "I didn't even want to sleep with you."

I arch my brows.

"Okay, well that's not true," he says and puts his hands into his jean pockets. " I totally wanted to sleep with you, but I'd never met a woman like you. In my entire life. I just wanted to be with you and I was afraid sex would mess it up. I told you that, remember?"

"I remember," I say softly.

"I wanted to tell you who I was so many times, but I was afraid."

I blink up at him. "What were you afraid of?"

"Of exactly what happened. That you'd think I was being an asshole, or slumming."

I wince as I think about the things I said to him. He might have been withholding information, but my words were cruel and meant to hurt, because I was hurting. I'm not really the kind of person to hurt anyone on purpose.

"I don't really think that," I say. The man had been nothing but sweet to me.

"You said it because you were shocked and I'd hurt you. I understand that. But I need you to understand, I was afraid of ruining what we had."

"What did we have?"

"We had something that was really good, Aly. Something that's totally worth fighting for. Something that only comes around once in a lifetime, and I pray to fucking God I didn't fuck it up. That you'll give me a second chance."

"Your life," I say and glance out the window. "It's not here. It's in Seattle and Boston."

He shakes his head, the frown on his face wrecking my fragile heart. "You're trying to push me away," he says and I realize he's right. I am. "You're afraid. Afraid that eventually I'll leave. Right from the beginning, you told me this was just sex, because even then you were afraid." His eyes lock on mine. "I will leave, Aly," he says and I falter a bit as my stomach lurches at that truth. He reaches out, puts his warm palm on my face. "But I'll always be back. Always. I promise."

"You do?" I ask, hardly able to believe what I'm hearing. Alek wants more. He wants what I want. Can I forgive him for lying? Does he deserve a second chance?

"You trusted me once, and I hope you can trust me again and trust that I stand by my promise."

I take a deep breath and let it out slowly as he stands there, pouring his heart out to me and asking for forgiveness and trust. "I trust you," I say, warmth, love, forgiveness and understanding invading my heart.

His face relaxes and he steps closer, invading my personal space. With his body flush against mine, he says, "I realize you can't come with me when I'm on the road, and I'd never ask that from you. You need to be here with your grand-mother, but maybe you can travel with me sometimes. Let me show you the world that you've always wanted to see."

"Alek…" I say, and sniff as tears fall from my eyes.

He reaches into his back pocket and pulls out a piece of paper. He holds it out to me.

"What's this?"

"It's my bucket list," he says. "Will you read it?"

"Okay," I say, not knowing where he's going with this. I unfold the paper, scan the list. "Alek, this is my list."

"That's because I want all the same things you want. I want to pick avocados in Mexico, I want to pick olives in Tuscany, I want to have sex in a limo."

"We kind of already did that."

"Then let's do it again." His smile falls. "I love you, Aly. With all my heart. Nothing matters without you. I want to be a good man, the man you need."

My heart crashes into my chest and my knees wobble. "You are, Alek," I say through a tight throat. "You are all those things."

"I want to live in this house with you, raise kids here," he says, and I glance at his list again, to see those things listed there.

My throat tightens even more. "We can't. There's an offer in on it. That's why I'm here. To sign the papers.

"You mean these papers?" he asks and pulls something from his back pocket. My legs nearly give.

"You…want to buy it?"

"For us, yes. If this is where you want to stay and raise our family, that's what I want too. But I do have a house in Seattle that I need you to do some landscaping on. A lot of the guys do. And there is something missing from my list, babe."

"I know."

"Remember, I added to yours. I want you to add to mine, Aly. I need to know you want the same things as I do." He holds a pen out and I take it from him. I drop into a chair and scribble on his list.

A smile splits his face when I hand it back, and he reads it out loud. "Honeymoon in Jamaica." As soon as the words leave his mouth, he drops to his knees. "I would have come to you sooner, Aly. But I had to make a trip home, and then I had to make things right with your grandmother," he says and pulls a small velvet box from his back pocket. I gasp when he drops to his knees and opens it. "It's my grandmother's ring. It's tradition in our family. But if you want some—"

"No," I say as a big hiccupping sob rises from my throat.

His face falls, worry and fear invading his dark eyes. His

hand shakes as he scrubs his face. "No? You don't want to marry me?"

"Of course I do," I blurt out. "I mean no, I don't want a different ring. This one is absolutely perfect."

He exhales and wipes his brow. "You scared me for a second there. Maybe I deserved it, though." He takes my hands and slides the ring on my finger. We both look at it for a second, then he climbs to his feet and pulls me to him.

"I love you, Aly. You have made me the happiest man on the planet."

"I love you too, Alek," I say, and bask in his love, the smile on his face, knowing this is the happiest day of my life, and it's only going to get better.

He picks me up and I squeal as he spins me around. My heart soars with all the love I have for this man, and his kindness, sweetness, his willingness to work around what I need in life. A noise on the front steps reaches my ears.

"What's going on?"

He laughs and sets me down. "Come on, let's go say hello to my family."

My jaw drops open. "Your family is here?"

"Some of them." He opens the door and I glance out to see Quinn, Jonah, Scotty, and Cason. "They're your family now too, and I'll introduce you to my folks, the rest of the team, and Tyler and his sisters when you're ready. Your family is going to be huge, Aly." Tears flood my eyes, and he puts a comforting arm around me and holds me tight. I soak in his warmth, his love. "But I have to say, you might regret it. They're all kind of annoying. Especially Quinn."

"Hey," Quinn says and whacks his stomach. As he lets out a loud oomph, Quinn pulls me in for a hug. "Welcome to the family, Alyssa. It's going to be a hell of a wild ride."

I smile at my new sister. "I can't wait."

AFTERWORD

Thank You!

Thank you so much for reading, **The Puck Charmer**, book 7 in my **Players on Ice**. I hope you loved this story as much as I loved writing it. Keep reading for an excerpt of **Single Dad Next Door**, book one in my **Single Dad Series.**

Interested in leaving a review? Please do! Reviews help readers connect with books that work for them. I appreciate all reviews, whether positive or negative.

Happy Reading,
Cathryn

Rachel

When my bedroom door flies open and crashes hard against the paint-chipped wall, I groan. "Go away," I say, my voice muffled by my pillow. Not that my roommates will listen, even if they can hear me. Heck, I could scream at the top of my lungs and it wouldn't faze them, much less send them running back to their rooms —not when the view outside my window is that *hot*.

Seriously though, sharing a house with four college freshmen is not my idea of a good time, not when I'm a senior and working my ass off to get into law school. But when I left NYU two months before the start of my fourth year and transferred to Penn State at the last minute, this place was all I could find—and afford. Ultimately, Penn State is where I want to do my law degree after undergrad. I just ended up here sooner, rather than later.

Someone tugs at my pillow and I open one eye to see Becca hovering over me. "Come on, Rach, he just took his shirt off," she says. "You're going to want to see this."

Why oh why did my room have to come with the best view of the hot neighbor's driveway?

"Thank God for this heat wave." Sylvie, roommate number two, fans her face with her hand.

I groan and curl up into the fetal position. I just want one more minute in bed without every member of the house in my room. "I. Don't. Care." Well, that might be a lie. I like looking at the eye candy next door as well as they do, but after putting in a late night at Pizza Villa—I seriously have to find a new job—I need all the sleep I can get before class.

"Jesus, would you look at him," Becca says, her voice a breathy whisper as she peers out the window. "Talk about slurpalicious. I could seriously lick that from head to toe, and back up again."

"Leave," I say on a yawn.

Ignoring me, Sylvie squeals. "He's going back into his garage. Damned if he doesn't look as good going as he does coming."

"But I'd rather see him...*coming*," Becca says, and they start giggling.

"Seriously. Are you both twelve?"

"Shh, he's back," Becca says and swats her hand at me, like I'm an annoying fly that needs to be shooed away.

I shift on my bed, not to get a better look outside my window. No, moving has absolutely nothing at all to do with the shirtless mechanic turning my roommates into dim-witted moths. The *only* reason I'm getting up is to herd these girls from my room, and if I happen to get a glimpse of the hot, tattooed, badass daddy next door, well...then so be it.

I rub the blur from my eyes and toss my pillow at them. "Get away from my window, before he thinks it's me." They don't need to know that the hottie's bedroom window is also across from mine, and that late one night, he caught me staring into his room as he walked around in nothing but boxer shorts. Heck, if they knew that, they'd camp out for the rest of the school year, and that was so not happening.

"Ohmigod!" Sylvie leaps back. "I think he just saw me." She puts her hand over her mouth and starts to giggle. Footsteps pound down the hall, announcing the arrival of my other two roommates. I shake my head as they come bursting in.

Kill. Me. Now.

"Is he out there?" Val asks, her big blue eyes wide and hopeful.

"Yeah, but he saw me looking," Sylvie says. Despite that, she edges back around to sneak another look. Megan hurries across the room, and goes up on her toes to peer over Sylvie's shoulder, trying to catch a glimpse without getting caught.

"Do you really think he killed someone?" Megan asks.

"That's the rumor," Val protests, though her tone holds uncertain convictions.

"Then why isn't he in jail?"

"Maybe it was self-defense."

"He's such a badass."

"He's good with his little girl, though."

"Bad Boy Daddy, now that's hot."

"Do you think he'd spank me if I was bad?"

Unable to put up with their incessant chatter and giggles any longer, I point my finger toward the door. "Out. Now."

A chorus of grumbles ensues as they all sullenly walk to my door. Christ, I'm getting that lock fixed, even if I have to eat ramen noodles for the next month.

"God, you're such a grouch in the morning." Becca shoots me a wounded look over her shoulder.

"Doesn't even have to be the morning," Val adds with a hair toss.

"You need to get your nose out of a book once in a while," Megan says.

"What she needs is to get laid," Sylvie informs them all, but her solution to pretty much everything is sex. Problem is, this time Megan is nodding her head in sad agreement as she follows Sylvie out the door.

"I can hear you," I shout after them. I shake my head and my mussed hair falls over my shoulders. "I'm still right here." As I stand there, dressed only in my tank top and underwear, a warm breeze blows in and slides over my skin, a late reminder that I'd opened my window last night before crawling into bed exhausted. Great. Not only could the hot guy working on his car see my roommates drooling over him, he could *hear* them as well. *And* they just announced that I needed to get laid. How freaking mortifying. I stomp across the room and yell down the hall, "And don't bother to close my door on your way out." As usual my sarcasm is ignored.

I give the door a good slam, which helps improve my mood a little. With a deep breath, I turn around, not to see my hot neighbor, but to close my window. No way do I want him hearing anything else that goes on inside this place, or get the wrong idea that I might want him. I don't. Not in a million years.

I'm completely off guys, trying to keep a low profile. After my ex-boyfriend turned violent and abusive, threatening to kill me if I went to the police, I snuck away under the cover of darkness and put several states between us. He was big and hard like my neighbor, his muscles born from rough carpentry work. Last year, when he came to do repairs on the house I was sharing with friends, I was flattered that I was the object of his attention. At first he was doting and attentive, but as time went by, he became possessive and controlling. I came to find out later, he'd had other charges against him from numerous other women.

Jesus, why am I such a bad judge of character when it comes to men. Oh, probably because my only role model had been a mean-assed, alcoholic father who drove my beautiful, caring mom to an early grave and me out of the house the second I turned eighteen.

If I try hard enough I can still smell the cheap perfume on his shirt when he stumbled in after a weekend-long drinking binge. God, how I hated those women he slept around with almost as much as I hated my Dad. Mom used to try to protect me from his disgusting behavior, but what hurt the most was how he dragged Mom down, aging her pretty face far too early.

My heart squeezes as I think about her. She was a good woman, but was too afraid to leave. Running is hard. I get that now. Not that she really had anywhere to run. Our only other relative was my father's mother. She's still alive, living in upstate Pennsylvania where my Dad was born. While she liked me well enough, when it came to Mom and Dad, she always took Dad's side. That's how it is with parents, I guess.

I lift my arms, place my hands on the frame, and lean in to give it a tug when the hottie slowly lifts his head. Our eyes meet, hold a moment too long, and I suck in a quick breath as heat zings through me—and dammit, it's not the autumn sun that has warmth pooling between my legs.

OMFG.

With a wrench clasped tightly in his right hand he stares at me, like we're in a goddamn Mexican standoff. I swallow hard, and will myself to move, but can't seem to tear my gaze away. Ah, what was that I said about dim-witted moths?

Close the window, Rachel.

While my brain struggles to call the shots, my body has other ideas. Ideas that involve staying exactly where I am and ogling the hottest guy I'd ever seen. Blue eyes, square jaw, a body I could play Plinko on, and low riding, well-worn jeans that accentuate bulges in all the right places, and holy hell, the man has a lot of right places. Want prowls through me, hitting every erogenous spot along the way.

Just shut the window already.

He shifts his stance and taps the wrench against his leg as he looks up at me. A small grin touches his mouth, and that's when I realize I'm half naked. *Please, ground, open up and swallow me.* After hearing the girls, he probably thinks I'm trying to lure him to my room, fix that dry spell I've been going through. I grip the window ledge tighter and slam it down, putting the brakes on my body's reaction, and shutting out six delicious feet of hard muscle and pure testosterone. This is so not what I need right now. Coffee. Yeah, that's what I need. Lots and lots of coffee.

I hurry to the kitchen and shove a pod into the Keurig. I pour milk into a cup and set it on the spill tray. As I wait for the coffee to percolate, I wander into the main level bathroom and glance in the mirror. I look at myself and try to imagine how I appeared through the blue-eyed mechanic's eyes. I see black smudges under tired eyes, boobs that only look big because I'm slender from work, school and lack of proper nutrition and rest. My hair is...wait... I grab a fistful of my curls and examine them closer. Oh, God, pizza sauce.

Could this day get any worse?

Christ, even if he did hear my roommates, I'm sure he'd never look twice at a girl like me—especially the way I look now. A guy like him probably goes out with women who are a little more put together, sexier. Although I have to say in the two months I've lived here, I've never seen a woman come or go from his place. Still, I'm certain a girl next door who always smells like marinara sauce and pepperoni isn't even on his radar.

Good, because I don't want to be.

The coffee machine beeps and I hurry back to the kitchen. I grab the mug to take a big sip. Heavenly. Desperate for a shower, to wash last night's work from my hair, I hurry back upstairs to my room, hot mug of coffee in hand. I check the time and grab my clothes. Giggles come from Sylvie's room across the hall as I dash into the bathroom. I turn the shower to cool, partly because it's just so hot in the house, and partly because I need to calm my overheated body down. I might be off men, especially big, scary ones like my neighbor, but my body and brain aren't working in sync this morning. Clearly my libido didn't get the memo when I left New York.

I stay under the needle-like spray longer than normal, needing an extra minute to clear my head. When the water turns cooler, I jump out, dry off, and pull on a pair of shorts and T-shirt. I towel dry my hair, then tie it back into a ponytail. I forgo makeup. Not only will it melt off my face, I'm not trying to impress anyone or draw any kind of attention to myself. Once done, I grab my purse, shove my textbooks into my backpack, and head for the front door, feeling a little more alive after the coffee.

The hot morning air hits like a slap in the face and I groan. It's October for God's sake. It's supposed to be time for pumpkin spiced lattes. This is more like beach weather. Mother nature needs to get her shit together. I glance at my watch, and judging by the time—thanks to an extra-long shower—I need to get my shit together, too. This morning I'll have to take my car to school, or risk being late for class. The walk to campus is long, around forty-five minutes, but I prefer it on days like today. I need to save my gas money for the colder winter months.

Since my driveway runs parallel to my neighbor's, I keep my head down, toss my backpack into the back seat and climb into the driver's side. Thank God the hottie is out of sight and I don't have to go through the embarrassment of facing him.

I roll my window down and shove the key into the ignition. I turn it, only for the engine to make some god-awful sound and stall out. My heart races quicker. Shit. Shit. Shit. Frustrated, I give the steering wheel a thump with my fist. This can't be happening. I need this car. Need to be able to depend on it if I have to run again. It might be an old junker, but it's all I have. I can't afford a new one. Heck, I'm on such a tight budget, I can't even afford to have this one fixed.

I take a deep breath, throw up a silent prayer, and twist the key again, only for it to cough and gasp, like it's dying a slow and painful death.

No. No. No

A tap comes on the roof, and I turn to see my hot—shirtless—neighbor with his arms braced over the door of my car. He leans down, his beautiful face close to mine. "Need a hand?"

"I...uh...it's not working."

Jeez, way to state the obvious.

He grins, and when I see a cute dimple that contrasts sharply with his chiseled face, I nearly swallow my tongue.

"Yeah, I kind of got that, you know, being a mechanic and all." As he gives off a bad-boy vibe that messes with my common sense, he grabs a cloth from his back pocket, and wipes his hands before leaning into the car, his head practically in my lap.

Holy fuck!

It takes everything, and I mean *everything*, in me not to grab the back of his head and shove it between my legs. My sex practically quivers at the visual. The girls were right. I do need to get laid. I bite the inside of my cheek to stifle the moan rising in my throat.

"What...what are you doing?" I finally manage to ask, and will myself not to writhe restlessly, and show him what a needy girl I really am.

He pulls the hood release, and the front end of my car jumps. His head lifts and once again his face is close to mine.

"Popping the hood." He angles his head, and his eyes narrow. "What did you think I was doing?"

Oh, I don't know. Maybe you were taking this opportunity to go down on me.

"Popping the hood," I say quickly, and try not to think of sex. Dirty sex. Take-me-up-against-the-wall kind of sex. Not that I know anything about that. Sadly.

His laugh is rough and deep as he walks around to the front of the car, and I unbuckle quickly. My legs wobble as I climb out of the driver's seat and follow him. He's grinning when I reach him.

"What?" I ask, my voice raspy.

He touches my cracked windshield washer cap, which I happened to repair all by myself. "Duct tape?" he asks, his voice amused.

"Tools of the trade, right," I say and try not to sound as breathless as I feel. A difficult task considering I'm standing next to a half-naked man that I want to run my hands all over. I mean I've seen shirtless guys before, but come on. This guy is like a freaking viking. He leans forward to fiddle with something, and the movement shows off impressive bicep muscles. I break a sweat as his closeness sends shudders of need between my thighs. Honest to God, the man is a work of art, and all I can think of is no-strings sex—something I've never done before. But that's crazy and reckless and so not me. Truthfully, if I knew what was good for me, I'd slam the hood shut and run in the opposite direction.

I'm about to do just that when he says, "Uh, huh."

"Is...is there something wrong?" Is that my voice? Christ, I sound like I'm whacked out on painkillers.

For God's sake, get it together, girl.

He rubs the scruff on his chin, and I step back, needing a measure of distance before I actually reach out and run my hands over all his hard grooves and deep valleys.

"Plenty," he says again and checks something else. I have no clue what he's doing. I only know that he looks as hot as hell doing it. As he leans over my car, my gaze slides to his ass, committing the way his pants cup his cheeks to memory. The guy could be in a jeans commercial, or better yet, a Calvin Klein underwear ad. I'm a girl, but advertising like that would have me one-clicking the buy button.

My heart hammers as he stands again. He turns toward me, but I'm far too slow to react. His eyes are piercing, almost a deeper shade of blue when my gaze jerks to his, and I can't tell whether he's thrilled or pissed to find me checking him out.

I step closer and look over the engine. "So, what is it?" I ask, disgusted with myself. I should not be fantasizing over this man.

He clears his throat. "I think the first thing we need to do is replace the spark plugs," he answers, his voice a little hoarse.

"Yeah, that's what I was thinking," I say, my head bobbing in agreement.

That grin is back when I look at him. "You know something about cars?"

I shrug. "Sure...and duck tape."

He laughs and says, "It's not..." he shakes his head. "Never mind. So, you agree then, that something's not firing right?"

Firing? Oh, things were firing all right, and lighting up my body like a goddamn Fourth of July celebration.

Damn him.

Damn Mother Nature.

Damn dim-witted moths.

Confessions of a Bad Boy Gamer

Confessions of a Bad Boy Millionaire

Confessions of a Bad Boy Santa

Confessions of a Bad Boy CEO

Hands On

Hands On

Body Contact

Full Exposure

Dossier

Private Reserve

House Rules

Under Pressure

Big Catch

Brazilian Fantasy

Improper Proposal

Boys of Beachville

Good at Being Bad

Igniting the Bad Boy

Bad Girl Therapy

Stone Cliff Series:

Crashing Down

Wasted Summer

Love Lessons

Wrapped Up

Eternal Pleasure Series

Instinctive

Impulsive

Indulgent

Sun Stroked Series

Seaside Seduction

Deep Desire

Private Pleasure

Captured and Claimed Series:

Yours to Take

Yours to Teach

Yours to Keep

Firefighter Heat Series

Fever

Siren

Flash Fire

Playing For Keeps Series

Slow Ride

Wild Ride

Sweet Ride

Breaking the Rules:

Hold Me Down Hard

Pin Me Up Proper

Tie Me Down Tight

Stand Alone Title:

Hands on with the CEO

Torn Between Two Brothers

Holiday Spirit

Unleashed

Knocking on Demon's Door

Web of Desire

New York Times and *USA today* Bestselling author, Cathryn is a wife, mom, sister, daughter, and friend. She loves dogs, sunny weather, anything chocolate (she never says no to a brownie) pizza and red wine. She has two teenagers who keep her busy with their never ending activities, and a husband who is convinced he can turn her into a mixed martial arts fan. Cathryn can never find balance in her life, is always trying to find time to go to the gym, can never keep up with emails, Facebook or Twitter and tries to write page-turning books that her readers will love.

Connect with Cathryn:
Newsletter https://app.mailerlite.com/webforms/landing/c1f8n1
Twitter: https://twitter.com/writercatfox
Facebook: https://www.facebook.com/AuthorCathrynFox?ref=hl
Blog: http://cathrynfox.com/blog/
Goodreads: https://www.goodreads.com/author/show/91799.Cathryn_Fox

Pinterest http://www.pinterest.com/catkalen/